D0449843

SAHARA
CROSSWIND

Books by T. Davis Bunn

The Quilt
The Gift

The Maestro
The Presence
Promises to Keep
Riders of the Pale Horse

The Priceless Collection

1. *Florian's Gate*
2. *The Amber Room*
3. *Winter Palace*

Rendezvous With Destiny

1. *Rhineland Inheritance*
2. *Gibraltar Passage*
3. *Sahara Crosswind*

T. DAVIS BUNN

SAHARA CROSSWIND

BETHANY HOUSE PUBLISHERS
MINNEAPOLIS, MINNESOTA 55438

This story is entirely a creation of the author's imagination.
No parallel between any persons, living or dead, is
intended.

Cover illustration by Joe Nordstrom

Copyright © 1994
T. Davis Bunn
All Rights Reserved

Published by Bethany House Publishers
A Ministry of Bethany Fellowship, Inc.
11300 Hampshire Avenue South
Minneapolis, Minnesota 55438

Printed in the United States of America

Library of Congress Cataloging-in-Publication Data

Bunn, T. Davis, 1952–
    Sahara Crosswind / T. Davis Bunn.
       p.   cm. — (Rendezvous with destiny ; bk. 3)

    I. Title. II. Series: Bunn, T. Davis, 1952–
Rendezvous with destiny ; 3.
PS3552.U4718S24   1994
813'.54—dc20   94–38348
ISBN 1–55661–381–4   CIP

This book is dedicated to
Samen Mina
A man wise in the ways
of both desert and city
A friend who hears the music
of the heavens

T. DAVIS BUNN, originally of North Carolina, spent many years in Europe as an international business executive. Fluent in several languages, his successful career took him to over 40 countries of the world. But in recent years his faith and his love of writing have come together for a new direction in his life, and *Sahara Crosswind* is his twelfth published novel. This extraordinarily gifted novelist is able to create characters and events for a high-powered political novel as well as touch readers' hearts with a quiet yet compelling story like *The Quilt*. He and his wife, Isabella, currently make their home in Oxford, England.

Chapter One

Sultan Musad al Rasuli's dungeon passage was foul with odors and centuries of agony. The jailer led the little group down the stairs, wheezing through lungs tainted by years of breathing the imprisoned air.

Behind him puffed the sultan's assistant, Hareesh Yohari, trying futilely to mask his nervousness by adopting an even more officious manner than usual. He cast a furtive eye back at the two Tuareg. The desert warriors followed close at his heels. Tall and hawk-nosed and cruel of gaze, they had been sent across the mountains from Marrakesh by Ibn Rashid, the undisputed master of Marrakesh's old city. Their orders were to make a final payment to the sultan, witness the demise of the prisoner called Patrique Servais, and return with the unfortunate's head.

At the passage's end the jailer stopped by a stout iron door. He rammed back the great iron bolt, shoved the door upon its complaining hinges, and motioned the other men through.

Hareesh Yohari stopped by the portal and announced, "The honored guests are to follow the sultan's jailer. I shall await you here."

"The sultan ordered you to be his official witness," hissed one of the men.

"Is not necessary, not in the least," Hareesh Yohari replied, drawing himself up to his full diminutive height. "The jailer will make a perfectly good witness to all that transpires."

The second man, darker and taller and far crueler looking than his minion, leaned down until his great beak of a nose was within an inch of Yohari's face. His voice was as quiet and dry and deadly as a desert wind. "The sultan said *you.*"

Hareesh Yohari swallowed with great difficulty. "Of course, if the honored guests wish for me to accompany them, who am I to refuse?"

Beyond the door stretched a great chamber, its alcoves and arched roof hidden in shadows cast by the smoky torches. The chamber was filled with hanging cages and vats and instruments of torture. This slowed down their progress considerably, as the two Tuareg showed great interest in all the implements, and the jailer responded to their queries with professional pride. Hareesh Yohari hovered just beyond the trio, almost dancing in his nervous desire to get the task over with and be gone from this foul and fetid pit.

Scarcely had they made their way through half the chamber before a great noise boomed, and the solid rock floor beneath their feet shuddered. The jailer started and dropped the red-hot branding iron he had been demonstrating. With a sizzle, it made contact with his sandaled foot. While he shouted and leapt about, the others searched and craned to discover the source of the noise.

A second noise, louder than the first, drowned the jailer's anguished cries. The Tuareg drew their daggers, the only weapons permitted them in the sultan's palace, and bounded toward the far wall, from beyond which the noise had come. They pulled futilely at the second great door. Then with an oath the taller of the pair raced back, plucked up the wailing jailer by his leather apron, and dragged him over. Hareesh Yohari scuttled fearfully along behind them.

As the jailer moaned and jangled his keys, a third booming explosion shook the chamber, this one followed by a great crashing and rending. Shouts resounded through the palace overhead.

The Tuareg buffeted the jailer with a pair of great blows before he managed to fit in the proper key and unlock the door. Together the Tuareg lifted the man and carried him down to where a final door stood between them and the sound of chains being plucked from stone and dragged across the floor. The jailer's hands were trembling so hard it took several further blows about his head before the proper key was found. The door was flung back, and with a great cry the Tuareg bounded in.

The chamber was empty. A ragged-edged hole gaped high overhead where before had been only a narrow, barred slit.

The taller Tuareg lifted the jailer with one mighty hand, placed his curved dagger across the man's neck, and hissed, "This was the cell of the one called Patrique, the one sought by Ibn Rashid?"

The jailer managed a terror-stricken nod. "I know nothing, masters, please, I—"

"Listen," hissed the other Tuareg.

In the sudden silence they heard voices speaking foreign words, then a roaring noise, followed by scraping, rending sounds. "A motor car," said the Tuareg.

"It can't be!" shouted a wide-eyed Hareesh Yohari.

"And ferengi are driving," the other said.

"Impossible!" Terror drove Yohari's voice up a full two octaves.

The taller Tuareg tossed the jailer aside and raced through the cell door. "To the ramparts, swiftly! We must signal to close the outer gates."

"Yes, of course, of course," the diminutive official agreed, but for some reason appeared in no hurry to follow them. "You must hurry, of course. And I must alert the guard. And the sultan, of course—he must know all."

But as the Tuareg raced through the outer dungeon, Yohari stopped, turned, and scampered to a small, hidden side door. He pushed the secret handle, slipped through, and quietly closed the door behind him.

Chapter Two

I t was the desert way.

Lieutenant Colonel Jake Burnes had heard that phrase so often from his tribal hosts that it had begun to echo in his mind.

For a week and a day he had walked through reaches so empty they had ached with their burden of void. And yet it was in this arid emptiness that his heart had begun to fill with appreciation for the men and women and children who allowed him to travel in their midst.

The Al-Masoud tribe were a people who defined who they were not by what they owned, not by their houses or jobs or ambitions, but by tradition. Theirs was an extended family of some eighty souls, bound to one another and to the past by centuries of tribal lore.

The desert way.

The phrase wafted through his thoughts as he stood on a rise above the camp, watching a heated discussion between the tribal elders and their leader, Omar. Even at this distance, their voices floated clearly through the desert air. Jake had by then begun to recognize Omar's style of leadership. Every major deci-

sion was first given over to open debate. But once the
judgment was set, any further argument was met with
savage fury. That, too, was the desert way, and for the
moment it seemed more real than all that lay behind
him and all that lay before.

So much seemed so distant here in this parched
land of sand and scrub and stone. The States, which
had birthed him and raised him and then sent him off
to fight against Hitler's forces. Europe, where he had
fought a war and fallen in love and forged the friendship with Pierre Servais that had brought him to this
vast desert. Even the mountain fastness of Telouet, not
so many days behind them, where he and Pierre had
breached a sultan's dungeon and narrowly escaped
with the prisoner and their lives. And faraway Gibraltar, the source of their telegraphed orders to cross the
desert at all possible speed with their recovered com-
rade and his important secrets.

All these places and events haunted his memory
and directed his plans. Yet somehow they seemed in-
finitely removed from his present reality.

A strange dark cloud hung low on the horizon, hiding the sinking sun and staining the landscape the
color of dried blood. Down in the camp, Jake saw a
brown arm extend from a sweeping robe to point toward the cloud, then another gesture toward the pris-
tine blue sky that still arched overhead. More voices.
More discussion. Nods of concern and knowledge and
understanding. The desert way.

Now he saw Jasmyn Coltrane detach herself from
a cluster of women and walk over to where he stood.

Jasmyn. He had first heard that name as part of a
bitter tale of treachery—the mysterious half-French,
half-Moroccan woman who was said to have betrayed

his friend Pierre for a Nazi officer. Then he had learned that her true story was one of love and loyalty and sacrifice.

It had been Jasmyn who helped them find Pierre's twin brother Patrique in the sultan's palace, who had arranged with her tribal kinsman to help them escape. And it was for her sake that Omar had taken them in and offered to guide them from the mountains outside Telouet to the Mediterranean port city of Melilla.

"There is a storm," Jasmyn told him, dark green eyes showing worry under her blue headkerchief. "A khamsin, it is called. A desert wind."

"So I see."

"It is tracking parallel to our course, but Omar thinks the night currents will turn it toward us. This is a risk we must prepare ourselves to meet, especially with the new lambs."

Jake had been up much of the night before, along with many of the others, watching the miracle of birth. Six lambs had appeared in the space of twelve hours. Within minutes of taking their first shuddering breath, the tiny animals had risen upon trembling legs and made for the udder. Their approach was greeted by a deep chuckling sound from their mothers. Little tails fluttered with the thrill of eating. Jake had stood with the others in the cramped paddock, watching and pointing and laughing with unbounded hilarity at their antics. And feeling lonelier than he had felt since beginning his desert journey.

Jasmyn touched his arm. "Jake?"

He looked down at her and confessed, "I was thinking of Sally."

"You miss her." It was not a question.

"Very much." It was a ridiculously inadequate answer. "It seems like everywhere I turn, I discover something new I wish I could share with her. Like the lambs."

"From everything you have said, I feel I know this woman Sally." Jasmyn inspected his face. "I have started a letter to her. I would very much like her to know how grateful I am for all you have done. If you give me an address, I shall be mailing it as soon as we pass a village with a postal system."

"I don't even know where she is myself," he replied sadly. "I have to send my letters in care of the U.S. Embassy in Paris. She's traveling around with some high-powered Allied generals. They forward mail by diplomatic pouch. But thank you."

"Poor Jake," she said, and reached over to touch his sleeve. "So much you have done for Pierre and me, and for Patrique. And now, when you need us most, we are so caught up in ourselves we scarcely speak to you."

"I really don't mind all that much," he said truthfully. In the distance, a whirling beacon of dust rose from the cloud's mass, lifting higher and higher, a fragile tower turned ruby red by the sun's final rays. "You and Pierre have years of catching up to do, not to mention an invalid to watch over. Besides, there's a lot to take in here."

"You like the desert," she observed.

"It's a world I never imagined existed," he said, "not in my wildest dreams."

"All the tribe are speaking of you," Jasmyn told him. "How a stranger has come and drinks in their world with his eyes. How he seeks to learn everything he can, do all he can, be as much a part of the tribe as he can."

She rose to her feet. "Come, Jake. We must break

camp and walk by moonlight for the cliffs."

The children were whimpering with fatigue when they arrived at the first great outcropping four hours later. By then the tribe had been walking with few stops for a day and much of a night. Omar pushed them as hard as he could, barking his worry at everyone, rushing back and forth, trying to ensure that neither animal nor tribesman was lost in the headlong rush for safety.

Suddenly one of the outriders hallooed from atop his camel and pointed skyward with his great, silver-clad rifle. Jake looked up with the others and watched open-mouthed as a coiling tendril of shadow drifted overhead. One moment all was clarity and a sea of silver stars. The next, a silent menace blotted out half the universe.

Omar's shouted instructions required no translation. Jake raced with the others toward the cliffs, which jutted out into the sand like giant sharp-edged buttresses. As they approached, Jake realized that the cliff face was pocketed with shallow, bowl-shaped caves. Eons of wind and sand had hollowed the sandstone into a series of natural chambers.

While the children formed a natural paddock for the bleating animals, Jake and all the other adults raced to raise three goat's-hair tents abutting a trio of neighboring caves. It was hard working by torchlight, men and women snapping in frantic haste and shouting words he could not understand. But by then he had grown accustomed to the task, pulling the heavy ropes taut and hammering down the ironwood stakes as long as his thigh. So he ignored the others as best he could and simply went about his chores, feeling the fitful breeze blow gritty breaths against his face and hands.

A great cry arose from several voices at once, and the entire tribe held its breath. In the distance Jake heard a sound that raised the hairs on the nape of his neck, a basso moaning that died away, then mounted to a force that left the ropes under his hand trembling in fearful anticipation.

At that the tribe doubled its already frenetic haste. Jake joined with the other men to mount a fourth tent, this one as a simple protective flap over a cave farther down the cliffside. The camels had both forelegs and back legs hobbled, then were tied in a long string to a series of stakes hammered deep into the earth just inside this protective awning.

The other three tents were joined side by side, fronting onto a trio of caves set close together in the cliff. The sheep and goats bleated in panic as they were herded into the left-hand tent, the one fronting the largest cave. By the time the double flaps were dropped and tied securely into place, the wind was growling about them.

Jake allowed himself to be herded into the middle tent, which was crowded with milling bodies. Normally they had twice the number of tents, and none used by animals, but there had been neither time nor nearby caves to set up more. Jake helped where he could as the others sorted themselves into family groupings. Lamps were lit and hung from supporting ropes. Carpets were unrolled to form a comfortably padded floor. A shallow hole was dug at the tent's center, rocks found and set in a circle, coals laid, a cooking fire started, a tea canister set in place.

Everyone paused to listen as the first great blast descended upon them, buffeting the tents with sandy fists. All eyes and ears searched the unseen spaces to either side, then gradually relaxed when it was decided that all the tents were holding well.

Within an hour the camp had settled into family groupings. Jake found himself a corner at the back of the cave, eased down on a pile of carpets woven in desert colors, and gave in to exhaustion.

The tribe slept a day and a night and into the next day, taking in sleep and storing it as they did water at the wells. Trips outside were battles against the wind and sand, and nobody went far, or for very long. Jake spent many hours dozing in solitude.

Once a waking routine was resumed, Jake visited occasionally in the third tent with Pierre and Jasmyn. But Pierre's twin brother Patrique, still weak and sick from his stay in the brutal Telouet dungeon, required much of their attention, and what was left they preferred to lavish upon each other. Their tent contained the old and infirm, the families with the very young or the very sick, as well as the unmarried women, and in quiet desert ways Jake was urged not to linger.

Jake found himself making numerous trips with Omar to check on the animals. The tribe's children spent most of their waking time there, filling the odoriferous tent with their delighted laughter. The newborn lambs were little bundles of black and white fluff. The animals frisked about, bleating their high-pitched cries, jumping and spinning in midair. Jake watched the children as much as he did the animals, marveling at how contented they were with the simplest of entertainments. They rarely cried or fought or whined, despite a life that was harsh by any measure. And here they were, cooped up in a tent with over a hundred milling animals, not a toy or a book between them, utterly content.

Jake found himself thinking that he, too, could be content in this sand-bounded desert world if only Sally were here with him. But the pain of missing her, which had dulled to an inner ache during the course of rescuing Patrique, now throbbed into anguish during the long hours of waiting.

When he dozed, he could see her clearly. Sally tall and lithe, cool and confident behind her desk in Badenburg. Sally strong and tender, kneeling to comfort one of the impoverished orphans the war had left scattered in its wake. Sally beautiful in the candlelight, her auburn hair gleaming. Sally sad but determined, telling him about her orders. Telling him goodbye.

And then he would wake to the reality of sand and wind and children and animals and Sally would be gone once more.

It was around noon of the third day that disaster struck.

By then, Jake had almost grown accustomed to the wind's continual growl. He was caked from head to foot with grit, and his hair felt like a used paintbrush that had been left to dry in the sun. But he watched the others and saw how they ignored what they could not alter, and he resolved to try and do the same. By the third day, the dry crunchy feeling of his skin seemed almost as natural as the thundering gusts that shook their tent from time to time.

The change came without warning. Jake sat cross-legged in what had come to be his corner, trying to concentrate as two men laid out a complicated game of rocks and shells on a board design drawn in the sand. He nodded as though he understood as they pointed at each rock or shell in turn, then gave lengthy explanations. Clearly they had decided that his lack of Arabic could be overcome by shouting, because their explanations were as gentle as artillery barrages. Jake found the game totally incomprehensible, but since they were tugging at his sleeve with one hand and fondling their daggers with the other, he tried to pay attention. He felt like his mask of wide-eyed interest had become glued in place.

Suddenly the wind's pitch rose to a horrendous shriek. The flickering lamps shook as the tent's guide ropes threatened to give. A terrific blast fought its way through the double flaps over the portal, blew out all the lamps, lifted up a great fistful of coals from the central fire, and flung them haphazardly about the room.

The tent went berserk.

Screams and shrieks competed against the wind's overpowering noise. The cramped space was instantly filled with jumping, whirling bodies, tumbling onto one another, tripping and falling onto yet more coals. Jake struggled out from under one writhing body, only to see the robe of a man next to him shoot up in flames. He tackled the man, tore up a carpet, and flung it together with his own body over the flames. Only when the fire was out and he raised to his knees did he realize the man he had saved was Omar.

Before the tribal chieftain could speak, another blast of wind split the night. In its midst came another sound, an explosive ripping followed by animal screams. Omar's eyes opened wide in the dim light and he shouted words Jake did not need to understand. The animals' tent had collapsed.

Somehow he managed to struggle across the mass of teeming bodies behind Omar and push himself through the tent's portals. Immediately the wind grappled with him, searching with harsh gritty fingers to pluck him up and hurl him against the cliffside. There was neither night nor day nor left nor right, only the golden-brown swirling mass that flung itself at him with such force that it threatened to rip the skin from his face.

Out of nowhere appeared a great looming shadow, one dusty brown shade darker than the storm itself. The shadow passed, to be followed immediately by another, and yet a third. When the fourth shadow appeared, Jake did not hesitate or think. He reached and found himself grasping at the sand-sodden hairs of a camel's neck. Somehow a string of camels had broken free of both their hobbles and their stakes.

The pelt ran through his fingers until he came to the thick harness guide rope. He grabbed hold and allowed himself to be flung from a standing start to a pace so fast that his feet scarcely touched the ground. With his free hand he reached blindly and felt a second rope trailing down from the camel's hump, the leader used to lash down the loads. Without thinking of the risk, he took two further great strides and flung himself up onto the camel's back.

The panicked beast was too busy running blind to bother with him. Jake struggled and managed to raise himself up and into the lumpy fold between the beast's double humps. He struggled against the jouncing gait that slammed him up and down and threatened to dislodge him with every step. Working his feet through the ropes running around and under the camel, he pulled his cape down far over his face and hung on for dear life.

Chapter Three

Although he did not ever really sleep, still Jake had a sense of awakening to the hush and the heat.

The wind and the camel's bruising gait had buffeted him to an aching numbness. Jake had been unable to unmask his face or hold his eyes open against the storm's blistering force. He had ridden scrunched over, his face pressed close to the camel's hide so that his hood was kept in place, blind to all but his growing pain. The jouncing, panic-stricken race to nowhere had bruised him from head to toe. Jake had hung on with the grim determination of one who knew his only hope of safety lay in not being tossed off. The enforced blindness and the relentless wind and the jolting ride had gradually melded together, until time had lost all meaning and Jake had been swallowed by a welcome nothingness.

Then he opened his eyes to a brilliant desert sun.

After three days of howling storm, the stillness was frighteningly alien. Jake struggled upright, wiped his eyelids with an inner sleeve, blinked, squinted, and laughed a hoarse croak.

The seven camels all wore remnants of their hobbles around their ankles. They were linked by halters, and dragged the uprooted staves as they cropped at meager desert shrub. The scene was so calm and normal it was funny, despite the fact that the cliffs were a distant smudge line on the horizon.

The camel upon which Jake sat was the only one with two humps. All the others had the more common single hump. Jake inspected them, doubted if he would have been able to keep his hold upon one of those.

He ran his hand tentatively down his camel's neck, fearful that at any moment the animal would recognize him for the novice he was and attack him with those great yellow teeth it was using on the shrub. But the camel paid him no mind. Jake snagged the rope attached to one of the staves, pulled it toward him, and grasped the wood. He leaned back as far as he could and tapped behind the camel's rear leg while trying to copy the "tch-tch" sound he had heard from the drovers.

Obediently the camel lowered itself in the slow rocking motion of a boat on high seas. When it was fully down on its knees, he croaked another laugh. Jake Burnes, camel driver.

With the motions of an old man, Jake half clambered, half slid down onto the ground. Keeping a very firm hold on the guide rope, he struggled up from his knees. Every muscle, every bone, every joint groaned in protest. His first few steps were little shuffling motions. His throat was too dry to permit much sound, so he had to make do with little ahs of agony.

Had the camels decided to desert him then, there would have been nothing he could do about it. But they remained motionless, save for the constant scrunch-scrunching of those grinding jaws on the dry scrub.

Jake shuffled up to the next camel, touched the back of its leg, tch-tched a second time, and marveled as the great beast obediently buckled down to its knees. Now that the storm was over and they had run through their panic, they seemed almost to welcome a semblance of their normal routine. He moved to a third camel and was met with the same dutiful response.

With the line now anchored by three settled camels, Jake began reshaping the line. First he untied the remaining staves so that they could not tangle about the camels' legs. Then he unleashed one halter at a time, leading the camels back and retying them so that the double-humped camel was placed in front.

After moving the three still-standing animals, he approached the center kneeling beast. Touching the stave to its side as he had seen the herders do, he gave a sharp "hup, hup," then jumped back as the neck swiveled around and the animal let out a deep, yellow-toothed groan. His heart in his mouth, Jake stepped forward, touched the side a second time, and hupped as loud as his dry throat could manage. The camel groaned another loud protest, but this time it lurched upright. Jake led it around and tied it in line, then did the same with the second kneeling animal. By then all six standing beasts were groaning in unison and stamping their pie-shaped flat hooves on the dusty earth.

Even though the lead camel still knelt in patient watchfulness, Jake had to use both hands to lift his leg up and over the animal's broad back. He too groaned as aching muscles fitted themselves back into the uncomfortable position. He tapped his camel's side, hupped a sharp command, then hung on and groaned again as the camel rose, its pitching motions reeling him back and forth.

But then he was up, high off the desert surface, with seven great animals groaning and stamping and waiting his command. He tapped his camel's side, hupped as loud as he could, and watched as the animal lumbered forward. He felt the line tug taut and begin moving behind him. Jake pulled his dry, cracked lips into a grin and raised the stave over his head with the sheer joy of getting it right.

By the time the sun began its rapid descent from late afternoon into night, the thrill had long since faded. Jake's entire body was one great thirsty ache. He had stopped trying to peer through the dimming light at the cliffs. Despite hour after hour of jouncing pain, they did not appear to have come any closer. Jake kept his head down, piloting his string of animals by their lengthening shadows.

Even with his eyes focused downward, they were almost through the patch of meager green before Jake's mind lifted from its fog of fatigue and thirst. He pulled on the bridle rope with what strength he had left and managed a single tched croak from a throat almost swollen shut. Thankfully, the camels appeared as ready to stop as Jake. At his tap the lead camel swung down in a motion so abrupt that Jake almost tumbled over. Once down, he found himself without the strength to lift his leg free. Jake gripped the camel's hide with both hands and slithered groaning to the cool desert floor.

Only the fear of the string pulling free and leaving him lost and alone in the desert vastness kept him from giving in to his fatigue. Jake scrambled to his feet, found himself unable to straighten up. Gripping the stave and hobbling forward like an old man, he walked to each camel in turn and touched them behind the knees. Three welcomed the invitation to kneel, three growled and snapped in his direction with their great yellow teeth. Jake was too tired to jump away. He responded with a raised stave and a hoarse growl of his own. The camels grumbled and turned away. Jake was more than willing to call it a draw and leave them standing.

The sandy earth revealed nothing large nor solid enough with which to pound in the staves. Jake was not sure it mattered, as he doubted he had strength left to drive them home. In desperation he noosed a second line around the lead camel's neck, then tied both ropes to his ankles. In the last light of a dying day, Jake checked the knots, then groaned his way down to the sandy earth and gave in to his exhaustion.

It would go down as the worst night in living memory.

In what seemed like only seconds after he had closed his eyes, Jake was jerked awake by the lead camel lumbering to its feet, grumbling its great guttural roar, then swinging about and trotting away. Dragging Jake along as though he was not even there. The rest of the string following as though a midnight stroll was the most natural thing on earth. Jake scrambled upright only to be tossed back with a thud. He gripped one of the ankle ropes, shouted hoarsely for the camel to stop, endured having his backside scraped across plants and rocks and sand and twigs, growing angrier by the second.

As abruptly as it had started, the camel stopped, dropped its great head, and began cropping on a bit of wild scrub. Jake scrambled upright, his chest heaving. He raised the stave, decided crowning an animal five times his size was not in his own best interests, dropped it, looked around, and wondered what was so doggone special about that particular scrub. The other camels were contentedly cropping away, paying him no mind whatsoever. Jake gave a single dry chuckle of defeat, lowered himself back to the desert floor.

And realized he was freezing.

With the sun's descent the temperature had plummeted. The flickers of night breeze drifted through his clothes like iced daggers. Jake drew his legs up, wrapped his arms around himself, and wished for fire. And thick desert tea. And blankets. And day.

The night was endless. Every time he drifted off he was jerked awake by the camel moving to another shrub. Jake slipped further and further into a dull half-awake state, suspended in a freezing netherworld of sand and fitful dreams and fatigue and aches.

When dawn finally arrived, Jake peered at the lightening horizon through grit-encrusted eyelids, scarcely able to accept that the night had finally come to an end. He used both hands to push himself to his feet, then shuffled over and tapped the lead camel behind its knee. The camel was as displeased with the night as Jake, for it rounded on him with a roar of complaint. Jake stood unmoving and watched the great teeth open in his face, too far beyond caring to be afraid. Clearly the camel realized this, for it retreated, grumbled, and sank obediently to its knees. The camel then endured a full ten minutes of Jake slithering and sliding and groaning until he managed to right himself on its back.

Hours into the day, the heat and his thirst and the unrelenting jouncing ride began to play tricks with his mind. Jake had an image of himself standing at attention before General Clarke's desk, pointing at a map and trying to explain just exactly where he was. Which was impossible, because the entire stretch of area through which he passed was blank. Across the empty yellow expanse was printed, "Demarcation Uncertain, Reliable Data Unavailable."

Next to the map stood a glass of sparkling ice water. Jake could not take his eyes off the glass, with the cold condensation rolling down the sides in tantalizing slow motion. Every once in a while the general would raise the glass and sip. But he never offered any to Jake, even though he could see Jake's mouth and throat were so dry he could not even swallow. Jake knew if he could just pinpoint his location, the General would reward him with a sip. But he could not find any way of telling where he was on that blank map. And the heat beating down on his head made it harder and harder to think.

The sun had passed overhead and was drawing a second set of afternoon shadows when the cliffs finally rose high above them. Jake bounced up and down, each step agony, and prayed with all the might his exhausted mind had left that he would not be forced to spend another night out in the open. Each breath rasped noisily through a throat almost closed by dust and dryness. His eyes were squinted down to sandy slits against the reflected glare. His legs and back burned as if branded. His arms were too tired to hold upright. His fingers were coiled loosely to the guide ropes. It was all he could do to keep from sliding from the beast's back and plunging in defeat to the desert floor.

A distant rifleshot crackled like lightning across the empty reaches. Jake jerked upright, then reached forward to pat the camel's neck as it snorted and faltered. Not another panic. Not now. He did not have the strength left to hold on. He searched the distance and saw five figures moving through the wavering heat lines, seeming almost to float toward him.

Another rifle crackled. This time the camel remained steady under Jake's hand. An instant of clarity granted Jake the chance to see that the figures were in fact sitting astride galloping camels and headed his way, rifles held up high over their heads. Another few moments, and he could hear their shouting and excited laughter. A sudden flood of relief washed through him. Tiredly he waved his own stave overhead.

He was safe.

Chapter Four

The tribe rewarded his return with great shouts of joy. Jake was pulled from the camel by a dozen eager hands, his back pummeled so hard his legs gave way. A bladder of water was thrust into his hands. After five days of resting in the distended animal skin, the water smelled foul and tasted brackish. Jake squirted a flood of warm liquid into his parched mouth, and thought he was feasting on nectar.

They ignored his protests and herded him up into one of the dark tents fashioned upon a larger camel's back, where the infirm and elderly normally rode. Omar came to see that he was settled in well and explained through Jasmyn that they must make all haste for the next oasis, as the waterskins were almost dry and the animals were growing too parched. Another day of walking in the heat would doom the weaker beasts. Omar knew exactly where they were, he said; the oasis was a five-hour march due north. They could follow the cliffs and the stars and would arrive near dawn.

The tribal chieftain then looked up at Jake's resting-place and said, "The tribe is most grateful for your acts of courage. For myself, I will hold my thanks until later."

Jake dozed much of the journey. The ocean beast rocked as gently as a ship riding over great rollers, and Jake's berth was made soft by layers of carpet. Overhead, the tent's cloth sides flapped with each swaying step, like sails set to snare the stars and power them through the dark reaches. The desert floor was transformed by moonlight into a frozen silver sea. The loudest sound he heard as he drifted in and out of sleep was the bleating of the animals.

The sky had not yet gathered enough light to banish the stars when they arrived at the oasis. Long before the camp came into view, however, the sheep and camels smelled the water. Their cries and increasing pace awoke Jake from his deepest slumber of the night. He pushed aside the tent flaps to breathe the crisp night air and watch as silhouettes of palms appeared on the horizon.

The sun was well over the horizon by the time the animals had drunk their fill and the paddocks and tents had been erected. Once the chores were finished and most of the tribe vanished into the shade for much-needed sleep, Jake reveled in a long bath. The oasis lake was shallow and sandy-bottomed and lukewarm. Yet the waters were clearly replenished by an underground spring, because now and then he would pass through unseen ribbons so cold they raised gooseflesh. Jake swam the few strokes from one bank to the other, feeling his parched skin drink in the liquid. He floated for a long time, his only company the ravens that populated the oasis.

Eventually he stepped from the water, let the sun dry him off, dressed, and walked over to where the two tribesmen watching the animals were having great difficulty keeping their eyes open. With sign language Jake showed how he had slept on the camel and then offered to take their watch so they could sleep. The astonished tribesmen bolted for their tents before Jake could change his mind.

That evening, Jake sat with his back resting against a date palm and watched as night descended. The easy day had done much to restore both his body and his spirits. He looked out beyond the scrub and palms to the great golden emptiness, a land ruled by heat and dust and hardship. It made their tiny island of green and water a jewel of incredible value, something to be treasured, a place of restoration and peace.

The tribe was preparing for a feast. Gradually all the tribe approached to sit or sprawl in a great circle. In the center, an entire sheep turned upon a great spit. One of the women prepared semolina in the time-honored manner, drying the ingredients in wooden bowls, mixing them by hand and stirring, stirring constantly. Her arms flashed a blurring motion, her tribal tattoos of vines and fishes denoting one who had been married into the Al-Masoud from some place closer to the sea.

The sea. Jake leaned back comfortably, tried to take his mind from the fragrances that crowded the night, and wondered what it would be like to see the sea again.

Jake observed the gathering tribe. He had come to see the desert folk as a closed lot, suspicious of all outsiders, even those who were granted entry by custom. Hospitality was offered only within the tight barriers of formality. The more he came to know the world in which they lived, the less he found himself minding their ways. The desert was a harsh teacher, yet he found himself valuing the few lessons he had already learned.

Tonight, though, there was a difference. Tribesmen stopped to offer him faint greetings before dropping to their places. Some even granted small smiles. Jake found himself treasuring them, knowing they were neither common nor lightly given.

Pierre and Jasmyn pushed their way into the circle, supporting Patrique between them. Like Jake, the French officer wore the tribal clothing of voluminous white desert trousers, embroidered white-on-white shirt, and light blue cloak. Jasmyn wore the royal blue djellabah of the desert women with elegant ease. With Pierre's dark, expressive features and her exotic, black-haired beauty, they made a striking couple. Their good looks accented the fragile condition of Patrique, whose sunken eyes and hollow cheeks made him a shadowy copy of his twin. It was hard to think of this emaciated, dozing man as the former bold member of the French Resistance in Marseille.

They eased Patrique down on a cushion, then took up places to either side. "The tribe is calling you a hero," Jasmyn said, settling down beside Jake.

"If I had taken the time to think," Jake replied, "I would have never grabbed for that camel. Not in a thousand years."

"I have often thought that is what separates the coward from the hero," Pierre mused. "Just one split second of hesitation."

To change the subject, Jake looked over to offer greetings to Patrique, only to discover that Pierre's brother had already fallen asleep. Not a good sign. Jake asked quietly, "How is he doing?"

"The stop forced on us by the storm has not been altogether a bad thing," Pierre replied worriedly. "He is not improving as I would hope. His ankles and his feet are hurting him."

"And he has a fever," Jasmyn said softly. "I suspected it before, but today I am sure."

Jake examined Patrique more closely, saw a pallor that not even the fire's ruddy glow could erase, and felt the chill of one who had seen war wounds fester and turn gangrenous. "This is not good news."

"I fear he will not make the trip without better medical treatment than Jasmyn and I can give him," Pierre agreed.

Jake mulled this over as the meal was served and eaten. At Jasmyn's urging, Patrique woke up and ate, but as soon as his meager appetite was sated, he forced himself to his feet. Jasmyn was instantly there beside him, even before Pierre could rise. Patrique motioned for Pierre to remain seated, bid Jake a quiet good-night, and with Jasmyn's help stumbled back toward his tent. Pierre watched him go, an enormous frown creasing his expressive face.

Eventually, Jake admitted defeat to the challenge of eating an entire sheep by himself and set his platter aside. He eased himself back, belly groaning, and smiled his thanks when a glass of tea was passed his way. He then turned to Pierre and said quietly, "It may be a good idea if you wrote down everything he knows about this traitor in the French government. Make sure the evidence is clear enough to stand without him there to back it up."

Pierre looked over and replied fiercely, "My brother will survive."

"Just in case our ways split up," Jake soothed.

Pierre examined his friend. "You have a plan?"

Jake nodded. "Just the bare bones is all."

"I find that reassuring," Pierre said, subsiding. "Myself, I have been far too worried to come up with anything."

Jasmyn returned to the fireside and eased herself down. "He is resting as well as can be expected."

"Tell me again about this guy in the French government," Jake said, "the one Patrique thinks is a traitor."

"He does not just think," Jasmyn murmured. "He knows. You have not sat with him, listened to him speak for hours about this man. Even his fever dreams are filled with the urgency of his mission to expose this traitor and bring him to justice."

"Monsieur le Ministre Jacques Clairmont looks like a snail without his shell. He made a name for himself as a politician, even when he was in uniform," Pierre said bitterly. "Adjunct to de Gaulle's military staff, rich, from one of France's oldest families."

"From the tone of your voice," Jake observed, "I get the impression you don't much care for the gent."

"There were rumors," Pierre replied. "Even an officer in the field heard such things. Of orders that made little sense to those who had to carry them out. Of decisions taken that cost too many men's lives."

"I know the feeling," Jake said. "Only too well."

"He stayed on in North Africa long after the remainder of the staff followed the European campaign northward. There were sound reasons for this—needing to hold someone there, especially when ground forces in Algiers were cut to the bone and all possible resources flung at the enemy in Europe."

"Which would have given him the perfect opportunity to line his pockets," Jake said.

"Patrique says he is both greedy and ruthless," Jasmyn confirmed. "A man who would do anything to increase his wealth and power. Anything."

"What is he doing now?"

"Deputy Minister of the Interior," Pierre replied, the growl in his voice drawing attention from all sides. "And adjunct to the President's cabinet. Perfect for a man such as this. Responsible for all transport, all distribution of supplies, all economic contact with the colonies."

"Powerful," Jake said.

"Dangerous," Pierre agreed. "He will do anything to protect his position."

"But is his position," Jake demanded, "great enough to warrant the American and the British taking such an interest in our getting back safely with Patrique's information?"

"Of this I had not thought," Pierre admitted.

"It's been on my mind," Jake said, "ever since we received that telegram from Admiral Bingham. If the army taught me anything, it's that the brass wouldn't go to all this trouble just for the sake of two officers. No matter how much we might think our own skins are worth." He shook his head. "I'd give you thousand-to-one odds there's more to this than we think."

Discussion halted about the campsite as Omar stood and signaled for silence. He spoke at length, gesturing from time to time in Jake's direction. Jasmyn's gaze turned with the others toward him. "I did not know you saved Omar's life."

"That's blowing things a little out of proportion," Jake protested, but already her attention was turned back to the tribe's leader.

"What is he saying," Pierre demanded.

"That Jake threw himself on Omar and put out the fire burning Omar's robes with his own body." She looked round-eyed at him. "Is this true?"

Jake shrugged. "I tripped over the carpet I was holding."

Omar continued speaking.

Jasmyn went on, "Omar says that afterward as he stood blinded and deafened and helpless in the storm, a string of the tribe's best camels thundered past. One moment you were there beside him and the next you had disappeared. It was only when he realized you had risked your life to save the tribe's wealth that he himself was forced into action. He managed to hold the remaining staves in place while other tribesmen erected shelter around the cave." Her gaze rested solemnly upon Jake, as did those of the others gathered about the fire. "To have saved the animals in the midst of such a storm is the stuff of tribal lore."

Omar motioned to a man standing beyond the fire. The tribesman stepped forth and deposited two cloth-wrapped bundles at the chieftain's feet. Omar then turned his attention toward Pierre.

This time it took a long moment before Jasmyn was able to speak. "He says that all the tribe have witnessed the love with which you accept a daughter of the desert and the wind and the wild reaches," she said, her gaze fastened upon Pierre. "No one could see this love and remain untouched. He says that you have done the tribe, and their daughter, great honor. This too should be rewarded."

Omar picked up the first bundle and passed it to Pierre. He unwrapped the oil-stained cloth to reveal a gleaming rifle. Pierre hefted the weapon and breathed, "A mitraillette."

"It is not fitting for a man to walk these reaches armed only with a revolver," Jasmyn continued, translating Omar's solemn words. "All who are accepted by the tribe have a responsibility to guard and protect."

Jake asked, "You know the gun?"

"Ah," Pierre sighed, checking the action, stroking the stock. "This weapon and I are old friends. Look, no safety. Instead, a trigger that folds up and out of the way. Ingenious, no?"

"Fascinating," Jake said, smiling in spite of himself.

"No single-shot mechanism, and wild as a frightened recruit beyond fifty paces. But it has the muzzle velocity of a lightning bolt, and a steady touch can hold the bullets to one at a time." Pierre hefted the weapon toward Omar and said, "Tell him that I am honored to carry such a weapon on behalf of the tribe."

But Omar did not wait for the translation. Instead, he reached down and hefted the second bundle. He held it a long moment and said through Jasmyn, "These were the weapons of my father, a great leader of the Al-Masoud tribe."

A murmur rose from the tribe as he walked around the fire to set the bundle at Jake's feet. Jasmyn interpreted, "My father would be pleased to see you so armed."

With numb fingers Jake undid the leather thongs, rolled out the covering, and felt the whole world focus down upon this instant. A dagger as long as his forearm rested in a leather sheaf dressed in silver, its haft formed by woven silver wire.

"These are on loan only," Jasmyn said. "They are part of the tribe's heritage and wealth. Still, this is an honor, Jake. A very great honor. I have never heard of an outsider being granted such a boon."

Omar squatted down in front of Jake, showed him how to lace his cloth belt around the sheath and then knot it through the silver loop before tying it about his waist. The dagger rested snug against his belly, angled so that it would not get in the way when he sat or ran, rising so that the haft pressed against the muscle over his lower rib.

Not waiting for Jake to respond, he stood and strode back to his position at the head of the fire. Jake forced his hand to reach out and take the rifle. It molded to his hand as though it had been made for him and him alone.

Pierre demanded, "What is it?"

"A Springfield .30-.03. One of the finest guns ever made." Jake worked the bolt, so smooth it almost slid on its own. The stock was layered with filigreed silver that shone in the firelight. "I've read about them. Never held one before."

He raised his eyes to meet Omar's gaze. "Tell him thanks. I don't have the words just now, so please say it for me."

When Jasmyn had translated, Omar said something with mock severity, which brought a chuckle from around the fire. Jasmyn explained, "Now that you are one of us, Omar says you should begin standing watch. Pierre has his brother to look after, but you have already shown your first concern lies with the animals."

"I'd like that," Jake replied.

"He was only joking."

"But I want to," Jake protested. "Tell him."

The announcement silenced the camp. Omar examined him, then shook his head. "Standing watch once in a while is disruptive," Jasmyn translated. "The routine must be maintained with discipline."

"Fine with me," Jake said, meeting the chieftain's gaze.

"Watchkeepers hold their position every third night," Jasmyn translated. "Punishment for any who sleep through duty is fierce."

"I want the dawn watch," Jake replied.

That brought yet another murmur from all who watched and listened. "That is usually the duty assigned to the youngest," Jasmyn said.

Jake could not have explained it, but for him the desert sunrises were very special. A quiet time, when the world belonged to him and to God. There often came a moment so precious and so fragile that even to speak of it might shatter the experience. So he simply replied, "Seeing as how I'm the newest man on duty here, I'd say that fits me down to the ground."

"It means a day two hours longer than all the rest of us," Omar warned. "There will be no time for rest between end of watch and breaking camp."

"Even so," Jake replied, "that is what I want."

Across the fire from where he sat, a suspicious old goat of an elder, the man who had remained most hostile to their being taken in by the tribe, rewarded Jake with a single curt nod.

Jasmyn told him, "You are fast building friends here, Jake Burnes."

Omar spoke at length, directing his words to Jasmyn. When he finished, there was another chorus of quiet approval from the gathering. Jasmyn said, "Omar has requested that I spend a part of every day translating, so that he may speak with you. He sees that your interest in the tribe and our land is genuine and wishes to reward you by teaching you of the desert way."

Jake searched for something to convey his thanks. "Tell him his gift has a value beyond measure."

Strong black eyes held him from across the fire. Jasmyn translated his response, "As does friendship between brave men."

Jake scrambled up the hard scrabble rise that separated oasis and camp from the cliffs. He had been awakened for his watch by a guard who had planned to step up quietly and then feign alarm. Jake's wartime reactions had served him well, and before the man could approach he had already rolled free of his cover, weapon in hand. The man had grunted approval and walked away, assured the camp would be safe in Jake's care.

Jake had stopped by the campfire to bolster himself with a glass of tea. After simmering on a rock close to the coals all night, the beverage had the consistency of liquid cement. The tannin was so strong the first few swallows sent shudders down Jake's frame and threatened to remove the first layer of skin from his tongue. But it succeeded in kick-starting his reluctant heart and guaranteeing that his eyes would not sink shut.

He chose his position well, far enough below the peak that he would not be silhouetted against the night, yet high enough to capture all the camp with one glance. He settled himself down on the flat escarpment, set his gun within easy reach, and began a slow, steady sweep of the entire area. A savvy old sergeant with whom he had served in Italy had taught him that good infiltrators were hard to catch moving, because they knew to keep their movements small.

Night creepers, the sergeant had called them. The best way to catch one was to commit the vista to memory, and then if a boulder or shrub or hillock suddenly appeared from nowhere, to go and inspect. Cautiously.

Jake was not by nature an early riser. Under most circumstances, he listed dawn patrols just a notch or so above getting caught by crossfire. But twice already he had awakened in time to step beyond the camp and become captivated by the unfolding desert dawn. The memory was bright enough for him to seek out the experience yet again and even to look forward to its being part of every third day. Strong enough to stay with him for the rest of his life.

He released the cloth button sealing his vest pocket and took out his small New Testament. The moonlight was strong enough for him to read the tiny script with ease. The silence was so powerful the words rang through his heart like thunder.

Every minute or so he raised his head and scanned carefully. The oasis was a sharp-edged shadow staining the silvery, moonlit plain. Animals shuffled and bleated quietly, their every sound carrying clearly across the distance.

Jake raised his Bible once more, then took another glance upward. He searched the vast river of stars, savored the brilliant clarity of the almost-full moon, breathed in the air's bracing chill, listened to the wind's gentle whisper, and counted the night as his friend. The desert world was vast and endless and alien. He felt enthralled by the vista, captivated by the night on display.

Jake sighed and wished once more for Sally, aching to share the moment with her. As Jake watched the first glimmers of dawn take hold he wondered if this almost constant yearning was a sign of true love.

Light came swiftly in the desert as though dawn were too fragile a gift to last for long. Yet no matter how fleeting, still there was a moment. A single ephemeral instant when all the world held its breath, when all creation lay open and poised and fresh and new. The light grew full and yet remained gentle. The camp was utterly still, the great reaches achingly open and exposed. He and he alone was there to know this moment, the only man awake in all the world.

Then the instant of breathless perfection was shattered. The sun rushed over the horizon and blazed with fierce pride upon its harsh desert kingdom. Jake shaded his eyes against the sudden onslaught and saw the first stirrings of life within the camp. He sighed, knowing the moment was gone, yet reluctant to release himself from the thrall of what he had just seen and felt.

He started to reach for his weapon, then stopped. As cautiously as possible, he swiveled about, an inch at a time. Yes. There it was. Some flicker of motion had alerted him, and now he could see clearly. On the cliff behind and overhead and to his right a head was raised, clearly silhouetted against the new dawn sky. And there beside the head a dark line protruded over the edge, far too straight and true to be anything but a gun barrel.

Jake sat in utter stillness, wondering if the intruder realized he had been spotted. Eventually the gun barrel was drawn back, and the head disappeared. Only then did he risk a full breath, rise to his feet, and scramble back down the hillock to the camp.

Chapter Five

Omar listened to Jake's report with the focused alertness of a hunting falcon. When Jasmyn finished translating, Omar called for the three elders to join him and the story was told yet again. Jake watched them digest the news in silence and then waited for the eldest to speak first. Jasmyn translated the old man's question as "How long a gun?"

"Hard to say how much of the barrel I saw, but I'd guess it was man-sized. And he had a ribbon or tassel or something dangling off the end."

Tension crackled through the group. Omar demanded, "He wore a large blue turban?"

"The color I couldn't tell," Jake replied. "But the headdress was broad and flat, yes."

It was enough for the senior elder. "Tuareg," he declared.

"Tuareg are desert warriors," Jasmyn explained to Jake. "Mercenaries."

Omar spoke harshly, and Jasmyn translated, "They were once a tribe like ourselves. Now they are jackals and vultures. No longer do they hold animals nor wells nor pride of their own. They are a scourge, killing the weakest men and beasts when they can. They take anyone's silver and accept any task. Nothing is too low for the Tuareg."

"It's us they're after," Jake said, and knew a sinking sense of defeat. He said the words so they would not come from Omar and the elders. "Maybe we should take off on our own. No need to put your tribe at risk."

But his offer was met with vehement refusal. "No desert hyena will stop us from our task," Omar replied for them all. "We know now to move with caution."

"You think they'll attack?"

Omar shook his head decisively. "It is not their way. Even if they were certain of your presence, the Tuareg would not attack the Al-Masoud. We are too strong. No, they would harry us like the vultures they are. But for now they are armed only with suspicion and greed. First they will seek to learn if we harbor their prey."

"So what do we do?"

"Prepare," Omar replied, and strode back into camp.

The mountains that paralleled their course were barren and bleak, shaped by wind and heat so fierce that Jake often heard rocks splitting open at midday. They cracked with lightning force, frightening the animals and causing the men to raise weapons and search the empty peaks. But not for long. Experience had taught them that few bothered to stalk the occasional traveler here so far from water. Greater dangers lay closer to the wells.

Jake walked alongside Omar and Jasmyn, trying to match the chieftain's long strides, falling into the rhythm of Omar's speech and Jasmyn's translation.

"Ours is the tribe of Al-Masoud," he said through Jasmyn. His voice took on a timeless timber, chanting words spoken by countless generations, teaching Jake as he himself had been taught. "We are known as the desert foxes, for those of us who wish can travel great distances at great speed and be seen only by those to whom we grant vision."

He stretched out his hand. "Ask anyone in the desert. They will speak of us with respect. No one has ever said a bad word of our tribe. We follow the command of hospitality. We give of our best. This is the way of honorable men."

Today the move was short, less than twenty miles. It was part of a yearly cycle that took Omar and his tribe across eight hundred miles of desert and mountain and sand and rock and scrub. The search for pasture never ended in this, their arid homeland. They walked and rode with all their belongings strapped to their camels' backs, and earned the right to stand with pride by the simple act of surviving.

"We follow the customs," Omar went on, his voice rising and falling in practiced cadence. "We respect our tribe and our elders. We love our children and our animals. It is enough. Dawns begin with prayers and the lighting of fires and the milking of animals. Milk and fresh curds are our lifeline. Our animals feed us and clothe us and grant us the products which we can trade in the cities. We show our gratitude by treating them well. Normally we do not trek every day. This we do for you. Normally, when the milk bowls are not filled at dawn, it is our animals' way of telling us that the grazing is poor and it is time to find new pastures."

Omar's commanding presence made him appear much taller than he truly was. Although he stood an inch below six feet, Jake often had the impression of looking up to him, especially when he was speaking. His features seemed carved from the rough red sandstone of the surrounding cliffs, his body lean and hard and sparse. His bearing was erect, his dark gaze far-seeing and direct, his voice solemn and sonorous. Omar was every inch a leader.

They tracked a narrow flatland that was bordered on one side by the sandstone Atlas foothills and on the other by the sand mountains of the Western Sahara. To either side the dry and looming shapes were as mysterious and beckoning as death.

"The sheep need water every three or four days," Omar went on. "The camels can last up to two weeks, but that is not healthy for them."

Jake nodded and heard not just the words but the message. Here the options were simple and stark, either water and life or thirst and death. It was a leader's responsibility to know every well, every seasonal creek, every sinkhole within a range of eight hundred miles. And in a world where sand mountains were carved and shifted overnight this was the task of a lifetime.

A young man walked two paces behind them, proudly leading Omar's camel with its high-backed, embroidered leather saddle. This duty was passed to each adolescent of the tribe, boy and girl alike, granting them an opportunity to walk with their leader and learn from seeing him in action.

"This has been a good year," Omar continued through Jasmyn. "The sheep and camels have been fruitful. There has been grazing, there has been water. Only two wells were dry, and one choked with the poison of salt. A good year. And your coming shall hopefully make it better."

"We will hold to our pledge of payment," Jake promised.

"It is good to speak with one who honors his debts," Omar replied when Jasmyn had finished translating. "But life teaches us to count the silver pieces only when they ride in the purse at our belts."

Jake nodded but didn't answer. He could feel himself storing up lessons with every breath, as he had little chance now to ponder them deeply. This life was too new and too hard to allow much contemplation. The land through which they passed was one vast anvil, the sun and the heat dual hammers that pounded constantly upon his body and his spirit and focused his energies toward survival. But still he knew, on some deep visceral level, that much was being taken in and stored for an easier time, when he could sit and reflect and understand.

If the heat and the trekking bothered Omar, he did not show it. With natural motions he swung his body in time to his strides, constantly checking in all directions, inspecting the outriders, the shepherds, the animals, the children, the women, the way ahead. Jake asked, "Where do we stop tonight?"

"Ras-Ghadhan," Omar replied. "A village of shadows, some of them our own."

In translating Omar's words, Jasmyn's voice took on a slight tremor. Jake glanced down. "Is something the matter?"

"My mother told me once of this place," she replied. "I had nightmares for many weeks."

"While my father's father was still chief and my father was still young," Omar intoned, his voice a chant as constant as the wind, "the droughts came and the animals died. We trekked from oasis to well to lake to oasis and found no water. Wells that had known water from the dawn of my tribe's history, a dozen generations and more, gave us nothing but mud and dust and despair. So we went to the village of Ras-Ghadhan. There was water and work and a moneylender who owed my tribe enough silver to feed us until the waters reappeared.

"Aiya," Omar sighed a painful breath. "The stories we gained from that city. The scars. Those are stories we shall ever wish to forget, stories we shall carry untold to our grave."

"His father's father," Jake mused. "It must have been, what, sixty years ago, and he talks like it happened yesterday."

"Every village and every tribe has a storyteller," Jasmyn explained. "Their job it is to make the past live again for yet another generation, to remind them of the great, the glorious, the sorrow, the traditions, the heritage. For these people, the past is not a half-forgotten legend. The past is as real and as vital as the present. It gives definition to both their lives and their tomorrows."

"The Tuareg are a people who were once like us," Omar continued, and Jake's head jerked upward at the name before Jasmyn had a chance to translate. "The drought came and they went to the city of Raggah, five days north from here. They, too, were scarred. Like us, they had the city's stories branded upon their hearts. But the Tuareg were not strong. It is only at a time like this, when the world strips away all that was, that a man comes to know his secret strength. The Tuareg had no well of strength to draw upon, so in the end they sold their souls to the city. Now they wander the streets. They slave at tasks meant for no man. They stoop in the market and argue for hours over a penny. Their lives are filled with words and money and city smells. The Tuareg, who were once like us, are no more a people of honor. They have been devoured by the city. They are shadows."

Omar raised his head and said to the empty desert sky, "The Tuareg are no more. Behold the danger of looking to the city when the drought comes. The Tuareg are no more."

Chapter Six

T he village outskirts were marked by the roadway becoming imprisoned. Walls of clay-daubed stone grew and enclosed them. After his time in the desert, Jake felt as though he were suddenly gasping for air.

Clearly Omar shared his unease. Through Jasmyn he said, "I for one will know comfort only when my back is toward this place."

"Then why are we stopping here?"

"Because it lies directly in our path," Omar replied. "If it was indeed Tuareg you saw upon the cliff, they will most likely seek to inspect us here, as this is a village to their liking. To avoid it would draw undue suspicion our way. And if they do appear, we will know with certainty that unwelcome eyes are turned our way."

The walled path narrowed further until two camels could scarcely walk astride. Through a sudden gap in the wall, Jake caught a final glimpse of the desert; as far as he could see in every direction was nothing but flatness and sand and sun and heat. Then the village swallowed them.

The hamlet was tiny by Western standards, smaller even than the grounds of a large Western estate. His hood drawn down far enough to shield his blue eyes from sight, Jake followed the others down the dusty way, past two small squares where women drew water from stone wells. He had the sudden impression that these walls had been built to protect the village's most precious possession—water.

The caravansary was a dismal affair, a litter-strewn walled plaza utterly barren save for a well and two bedraggled date palms. Their only way in or out was by a narrow passage leading back through the heart of the village. Jake watched Omar bow and salaam to the village elders who hurried over, and knew he would sleep with one eye open that night.

Taking water from another tribe's well meant more than an hour of negotiation. All that while, beasts and children bellowed from thirst, pressing Omar to make a hasty bargain. But he was a man of strength and patience and did not turn away until he was satisfied with the deal.

Jake helped raise the water by harnessing camels to long ropes and drawing up skin after skin, which was then tipped into metal cisterns. As always, the animals drank first, then the people. When it came his turn, Jake bent over the cistern to wash his face, and was startled to find a German air-cross staring back up at him; the cistern had been fashioned from the wing of a downed fighter plane. He carried that thought with him as he helped erect the animal paddocks. Here in the desert, nothing was wasted. Nothing.

Omar walked over holding a bloodstained bandage. Through Jasmyn he explained, "Wear this about your forehead, and if we are approached you must draw the edge down over one eye, and keep the other in the bandage's shadow."

Gingerly Jake accepted the cloth and inspected the red stain. "Who wore this last?"

Omar granted him a small smile. "Even the sheep make sacrifices to keep you safe."

His chores finished, Jake joined the other men by the smaller cooking fire. Omar himself saw to the little teakettle and the leather bag of sugar, pouring out thimblefuls of black, highly sweetened tea, making sure each man had his glass before serving himself.

Traditions like this ruled the tribe's daily existence, offering a framework for living in this harsh and desolate land. This time before the evening meal was always a moment of peace and satisfaction. The tribe had been brought safely through another trek, there was food, there was water, there was safety. Now was the time for talk.

The day was dissected. The animals would be discussed one by one. It was the one time of day when the men spoke with ease, without guarding each word as they did their animals. Jake stood with the others, listening to words he did not understand, watching the tribe's life unfold and fill even this bleak little square.

The women were beautiful, their features as clearly defined as the desert shadows. Their skin was the color of honey, their eyes dark and fathomless. They wore the traditional black headkerchief, but most kept their faces open to the wind and the sun in the Berber fashion.

The first tent poles were struck with an invocation to Allah the merciful, the compassionate, to shield them in this their home for one night. Curved hoops were set in the earth, then great sand-colored sheets were slung up and over and tied in place. A woman sang a haunting melody as she unfurled the great tent's sheet. Her voice rose and fell in a cadence timed like a camel's steps, her words as lilting as a desert wind at dawn.

While the meal was prepared, the children lined up before one of the aged grandmothers. The children's heads were shaved once a week. The grandmother used a flat razor blade, kept in a special pouch. She entertained them with a story as her hand scraped, scraped, scraped away at their dark locks. If the children began howling when the razor was brought out, their cries were the signal that it was time to barter for another blade.

Jake made hand signals requesting two full glasses of tea, then carried them over to where Pierre sat with Patrique. They were stationed at the opening of the tent farthest from the narrow entranceway. With his dark eyes and his features worn by days in the desert, Pierre could easily have passed for a member of the tribe.

Jake worked to keep a smile from his face as he squatted down and offered the two glasses. "Nice to see you looking so fit, Patrique."

One hand emerged from dark folds to accept the glass. "I am hot and I am uncomfortable. It is not proper to make jokes at one so trapped."

"Sorry. You've got to admit, though, the outfit does have a lot going for it."

Before entering the village, Patrique had reluctantly accepted Omar's orders and donned the garb of an elderly woman—black djellabah draped from head to fingertips to toes. The hunters would be searching for one with scars on ankles and wrists. The only person safe from such inspection would be a woman. It would also be easier to hide Patrique's evident weakness behind the dark head-scarf.

Jake pointed to the pen and paper in Pierre's lap. "I didn't mean you had to do it all the time."

"I insisted," Patrique said. "It is good insurance, in case—"

"Stop," Pierre ordered sharply.

Patrique drew back the head-scarf and sipped from his glass, his hand trembling slightly. "Pierre tells me you have a plan."

"Maybe." Jake settled on the ground in front of them and began talking. The three of them were soon so intent on the discussion that they did not notice Jasmyn's approach. But when Jake finished, she was the first to speak. "It is a good plan, Jake. I think it will work."

"I don't like it," Pierre declared.

"Which would you prefer, my brother?" Patrique asked, his eyes glittering with feverish intensity. "Either we accept the fact that some action must be taken, or I shall be laid to rest here in this land."

"Do not speak like that," Pierre said. "I forbid it."

"Forbid all you wish," Patrique replied. "But it will not change the fact that I cannot continue much farther."

"He is right, my beloved," Jasmyn agreed.

"Listen to your woman," Patrique urged, the effort of seeking to convince his brother bringing a clammy sweat to his forehead. "Twice already she has saved my life. Three times, if you count her part in the nightmare of Telouet. She knows, Pierre. I cannot go much farther."

"But to split up," Pierre protested, weakening.

"Someone must carry on," Patrique said. "This

news must be passed on to those who can stop the madness. Think, my brother, I beg you. We owe this to all who have fought and died to make France free once again. We cannot stand aside and allow her to become imprisoned by other dark forces."

Jake sat and watched as the internal struggle was mirrored on Pierre's mobile features. But before he could speak, the normal rhythm of the tribe faltered. There was nothing marked, nothing to which Jake could point and say, here, this is what I noticed. Yet the time in the desert had sharpened his awareness, and he knew without understanding exactly why that danger had entered into their midst.

The others noticed it too. Patrique dropped the dark head-scarf over his features. Pierre rose smoothly to his feet, the mitraillette suddenly appearing in his hand. Jake paused long enough to veil his gaze with the bloody bandage, then stood and turned toward the entranceway, his hand on the knife at his waist.

There were three of them. The central figure was sleek and self-assured and wore fine robes woven with threads of silver. The other two were obviously men of the desert, but the difference between them and the Al-Masoud could not have been greater. In place of strength and quiet pride, their faces held only cynical cruelty.

Jasmyn slipped up close behind him and Pierre and whispered, "The central one is a trader."

Pierre whispered back, "The others?"

Jasmyn replied with the single word, "Tuareg."

Omar approached and salaamed formal greetings. The trader bowed low, his left hand sweeping up the folds of his robe while the right touched heart and lips and forehead. The Tuareg stood and glared and said nothing. Taking no notice of the pair, Omar led the trader over and motioned for him to be seated on a carpet rolled out ceremoniously by the central fire. The Tuareg followed with an insolent swagger, their dark eyes sweeping the camp.

When the trader had settled, Omar remained standing, and for the first time he looked directly at the taller of the Tuareg. There was no change to his features, but the challenge was clear. Omar extended a hand, half in invitation, half as an order, for the Tuareg to take seats by the trader. Clearly this was not what the Tuareg wished.

As the pair locked eyes and wills, Jake looked from one to the other and glimpsed the two paths taken by these men and the tribes they represented. Upon Omar's features were stamped the strength and power and determined focus of one who lived by honor and traditions. The Tuareg's features were little different from Omar's, with the same hawk nose and fierce dark desert eyes, yet the Tuareg's face was shaped by unbridled cruelty.

The tension mounted until the entire square was held in the grip of the silent standoff. Then the Tuareg snorted his derision, and settled down upon the carpet. Only when the second man had also seated himself did Omar take his place by the trader and motion for tea to be brought.

The trader spoke with rolling tones and florid gestures. Jake did not need to understand the words to know this was one who lied with the ease that others draw breath. As he watched the discussion proceed with formal precision, Jake could feel the danger heighten his perceptions.

He looked from Omar to the trader to the Tuareg

and back again. Here, he sensed, was an important truth. Something essential about the desert life was displayed here before him. This was why the tribe clung so determinedly to their traditions and their lore. The desert's harshness was always there, ever ready to steal away the moral fiber that bound them together. As Jake stood and watched and listened to words he could not understand, he knew a pride for Omar and these people, an affection so strong that the flame burned his chest.

Omar turned and gestured to one of the men standing behind him. A moment passed before several of the tribe stepped forward and unrolled richly colored carpets. Jake had watched the old women weaving these, working as they traveled upon the camels' backs and sitting by the fireside in the evenings, chattering and laughing among themselves, their hands never ceasing their nimble dance. In the sunset's burnished glow, the carpets' rich red and orange hues shone as though lit by a fire of their own.

The trader glanced casually down at the offered rugs and then swiftly turned away, continuing with his elaborate talk. Others stepped forward and set upon the carpets more of the tribe's handiwork—hair and hides of desert goats fashioned into waterskins and tent coverings, and lamb's wool spun into soft blankets and vests for the cold desert nights. Again the trader paid them scant mind, seemingly lost in his conversation.

With formal correctness, Omar hefted a belted vest, the stitches worked with brilliant thread and patterned after the flowing Arabic script. He ran his hand over the rich wool and spoke in a voice that did not require volume to demand a response. Reluctantly the trader cut off his flow of words and accepted the vest. He picked at the wool, frowned with theatrical concern, then spoke a few words.

With a speed that surprised them all, Omar was on his feet, lifting the trader by one arm and gesturing for the wares to be taken back and stored away. The trader yelped in protest, clearly having been prepared for hours of bargaining. But Omar was having none of it. Polite yet determined, he signaled that the discussion was at an end.

Recognizing that this was not a ploy, and seeing the wares vanish from view, the trader yelped a second time. Omar replied by silently waiting and watching as the two Tuareg rose to their feet. The trader plucked at his sleeve, smiling nervously, reaching out into the gathering night toward where the wares had vanished.

Suddenly the Tuareg were less interested in the argument than they were in examining the camp's periphery. Jake felt their gazes rake across him, pass on, then return for a second inspection. He forced himself to stand still and unflinching. But only when the gaze moved onward was he able to draw breath again.

The taller mercenary stepped away from the fire as though wishing to enter deeper into the camp. Instantly a phalanx of tribesmen were there to bar his way. The Tuareg snarled a curse. The trader moved forward and spoke with eyes closed to cunning slits, his eyes now on the animals paddocked at the square's far end. Caught in a quandary, Omar hesitated only a moment before waving for the tribesmen to let them pass.

A passage opened, barely wide enough to permit one visitor to pass at a time. The trader stepped forward, a nervous giggle escaping under the pressure of the tribesmen's stares. The Tuareg swaggered after him, hands on knives, their eyes sweeping back and forth through the camp as they walked.

At the paddock, the trader went through an elaborate charade of inspecting several animals before speaking a question. Omar responded with a single snort of humor and jerked his head upward in the desert signal of negation.

The trader spoke again, his voice rising. Omar replied by steering the man about and directing him toward the square's entranceway. The tribesmen closed in about them, forcing the Tuareg to follow. Seeing that his protests were to no avail, the trader gathered himself, flung his robes up and about his left arm, gave Omar a single cold nod, and stomped off.

Only when they had left the square did Jasmyn venture to speak. "Omar refused to deal with him."

"I understood that much," Jake said, and discovered that his voice was as shaky as his legs from the aftershock of passing danger.

"Omar accused him of offering prices meant for those who had returned from unsuccessful trading at Raggah. But since we are headed there, we shall simply wait and trade in the souq ourselves."

"Raggah," Jake said. "Isn't that the city where the Tuareg live?"

Before she could reply, Omar walked over and spoke. Jasmyn translated, "Danger has passed for the night."

"That trader was a piece of work," Jake said.

"Indeed, a man so oily he could escape the tightest shackles," Omar agreed. "He also talks too much. In the desert way, we say that here is one who scolds the trees. When the trees do not answer, he scolds the stars. But we say there remains hope, so long as he scolds only the made things, rather than the Maker. Before, I thought there was hope for this one. Now that I see him in the company of vultures, I am no longer certain. It is doubtful that we shall trade with him again."

Jake asked, "Is it true we are headed for Raggah?"

"It is the natural destination of all on our course," Omar explained. "To the west are mountains without passes. To the east, desert without water. All who go north must stop at the oasis of Raggah."

"Will we be safe?"

"The danger will be no greater there than elsewhere. There is a small French garrison, or there was the last time I passed. The war drained it to a symbolic force of three or four, but still the French soldiers held the Tuareg from doing their worst."

Jake glanced Pierre's way and said, "Better and better."

Pierre stepped forward and said, "Ask him if there is any chance that we might find medicines in this village."

"Doubtful," Omar replied. "The nearest healer is in Raggah. But I am going now to the village tea house to sit and listen and see what I can learn. I shall see if the merchants have anything. This is for your brother?"

"He is growing worse," Pierre said, concern creasing his features.

"This is not good. The way to Melilla is long yet. And the healer of Raggah will not be one to trust overmuch."

Pierre turned to gaze thoughtfully at Jake, then reached some internal decision and gave a single nod. "Please tell Omar we are sorry to have brought peril upon him and his people."

"The Al-Masoud are men of honor," Omar replied.

"We would not pass a cur into the clutches of the Tuareg."

"Even so," Pierre went on, "we are indebted to you and your people. Our duty shall continue long after the money has been paid."

Omar gravely accepted the translation, inspected Pierre for a long moment, then said, "It is good to know that one such as yourself is to wed one of our own. Long after you have departed, we shall remember that our daughter's husband is a man close to our hearts."

Chapter Seven

J ake awoke the next morning to the comfortable
sound of coffee being pounded in the tribe's brass
mortar. The young girl timed her strokes to the song
she sang, a warbling melody that pealed like bells in
the still air.

Breakfast was the same as every morning—treacly
thick coffee, dates, unleavened bread, milk curds, and
honey. Jake took his portion over to the side wall, drew
out his Bible, and read as he ate. The sounds of the
camp awakening were a reassuring chorus, familiar
enough now not to draw his attention. The children
laughed and scampered in scarce moments of playtime
before the chores of breaking camp were begun; camels
bellowed and complained as they were made to kneel
and the saddle blankets were set in place; a group of
men knelt toward Mecca and murmured their morning
prayers; several of the older women sat and spun silky
goat's hair with blinding speed, their mouths open and
gossiping and laughing in the morning sun.

The village *kunta*, a nomadic spiritual leader, arrived and passed from person to person. He made tal-
ismans, said the special healing prayers, taught a few
new verses from the Koran, and offered the traditional

blessings for good grazing and much water. His final blessing was the special one, offered for a safe and healthy passage through the desert reaches. Each person in turn held out their right hand, which was first touched by the kunta's cane, then spat upon. The nomads then wiped the spit over their faces and down the front of their robes.

Omar gave the call to break camp. Jake rose, tucked away his Bible, and joined the others. Again he had the sense of gathering lessons, storing up information and knowledge and newfound wisdom but being unable to digest what he was learning. Even so, he felt a sense of rightness to it all, a knowing on some deeper level that this need to sit and reflect would be granted him at the proper time.

When they had left the village and its confines well behind, Omar sent word for Jake and Jasmyn to join him. As the two of them walked toward the head of the caravan, Jasmyn said, "Pierre agrees with your plan."

Jake nodded, too full of sudden doubt to be very pleased. "How is Patrique?"

"There were no medicines in the village. Did you see him try to mount the camel?"

"Yes." It had taken three tries and the aid of both Pierre and Jasmyn to get him into the saddle-tent.

"Pierre walks with him now, writing whenever he has strength to speak." Jasmyn shook her head. "I hope your plan works, Jake."

"So do I."

"Even Pierre feels it is our only hope to save him now."

As they approached, Omar said to Jake, "Several

mornings now I have seen you separate yourself and read from a book you carry."

"It is a Bible, the holy Book," Jake said, answering the implied question.

"It is good for man to be bound by the custom of his religion," Omar said.

"It is more than that," Jake said, seeking a way to explain that would invite and not offend. "This is the story of Christ, the Son of God. His is a story of salvation for all who choose to believe. And His lessons are those of love."

Omar walked ahead in silence for a time, then said through Jasmyn, "Yesterday I sought to teach you of our ways. Today I would ask a question of you, a man of the world who speaks with wisdom of his own and who does honor to our desert ways."

"I would be honored to help," Jake said, "if I can."

"I have heard of this Christian god," Omar said. "There is a school now in Colomb-Bechar, five days march from Raggah. It is run by families who claim to serve this god of yours."

"We call them missionaries," Jake offered.

"I have two of the tribe's children, a boy and a girl, who beg to go and learn. Day and night they are after me. Even when they do not speak, still I can hear their little hearts crying through their eyes." He looked at Jake. "Sending a child to school means losing a herder. I must also pay for a family to keep them. While they are gone, their own mother's heart remains empty. A young boy's bed goes cold with his absence. A father misses the songs that his lovely daughter sang to the waking day."

"They might return and enrich the tribe with what they have learned," Jake ventured.

"Yes? You think this school will make them better people? That their lives will be better? Yes? Then tell me. What will they know, my children, that has enough value to wrench them from the heart of my tribe?"

"They will know languages. History. Math."

"Already they know their father's tongue. They learn the history of their father's father and their fathers before them. They can count their sheep and their goats. What more will they know?"

"They will know the world."

"No!" Omar pounced upon Jake's words. "They will know *your* world, not mine. They will know *your* knowledge. And then whose child will they be, yours or mine?"

"Everything you say is true," Jake agreed, marveling anew at the man who strode along beside him. "There is a risk that they will choose not to return. But what right do you have to refuse them their heart's desire?"

Omar subsided. "You speak a truth that has echoed through my nights since learning of this school. This is a question for which I have yet to find the answer. Tell me, man of the world who honors our desert ways. What would you do if you were faced with such a dilemma?"

"Pray," Jake said simply. "Pray and wait for guidance."

They walked for a time in companionable silence until Omar said, "I want my children to know the value of wisdom, but I also want them to know the wealth of the desert. I want them to have the city and the wider world to call upon when there is drought, but I want them to return to the desert in the rainy season. Is that so much to ask?"

"No," Jake replied, liking him immensely.

"Our world has changed," Omar declared through Jasmyn. "For many past seasons we stood upon our desert hills and watched the thunder of war from distant lands coming ever closer. No matter how far into the desert we went, still guns split the heavens and called to all the world that a new time was upon us. It does not matter what I like or what I wish. The seasons change, and only a fool refuses to accept what is."

He drew himself up to his full height. "But I am still leader of the tribe. And as leader it is my duty to see that the desert's wealth and wisdom is not lost. We shall change, yes. But we shall take with us what is ours. What others do not see, do not know, and cannot understand. What makes us who we are."

"It is a worthy aim," Jake said, and meant it with all his heart.

"I am a man of the desert," Omar said. "The desert is all I know."

"But you know that well."

"I know the wind," Omar went on. "I know the great emptiness that is as close to death as a living man can ever know. I know the feel of rock and the smell of water. I know the dry mountains. I know the dusty graves of ancient rivers. I know . . ."

"You know," Jake murmured, thinking of all he had learned.

"*Aiwa*. I know. And yet this, this is a new thing. A thing of wars and machines and cities. This new thing I do not know. And I do not know what is to be done. Not for today, not for tomorrow, not for all the days yet to be granted my people."

"Perhaps," Jake ventured, "perhaps you could find this answer also in prayer."

"Yes? You think this Christian god might turn to help a man of the desert?"

"He has promised to be there for all who seek Him," Jake replied. "All men, all nations, all times. A God who seeks only to give peace and love and salvation. To all."

That day they entered the area known as Zagora. Most of the desert through which they had passed was rock and shale and hard and flat, bordered by mountains and great, billowing desert hills. But Zagora was a region of sand. Oceans of drifting, golden sand. Gradually the Atlas foothills turned and moved away, leaving them enclosed by endless sand. Ever-changing, always the same. Hills and valleys and great, ghostly shapes that lasted only until the next great wind.

It was hard going for all but the camels, whose great wide hooves splayed out flat and kept them from sinking down. For the others, each foot dragged, every step sucked from the blistering sand. By midday, even the nimble-footed goats were complaining.

They walked nine hours with only two short breaks, yet managed only six miles. Jake knew this only because Omar told him. Distance meant little in this barren world. For a while that afternoon, as they struggled onward, Jake had wondered if perhaps Omar had led them astray. Each crested sand dune revealed nothing in any direction but more sand, more undulating hills, more heat. There was no track whatsoever, no road signs, no directional markers, nothing with which to determine either progress or bearing.

But then, as the sun began its grudging descent, a paint-daubed thorn tree came into view. All the tribe offered loud cries of relief and pride that Omar the desert chieftain had led them correctly yet again.

Around the thorn tree spread scattered desert scrub on which the animals could feed. It was the first vegetation they had seen all day. Jake helped form the paddocks with shreds of wood bleached white as old bones, then gathered with the others for the customary evening tea. There was no firewood; by tradition the bits of wood kept at the site were to be used only as paddocks. Their tea and the evening meal would be cooked over portable stoves, a necessity that everyone loathed because it left everything tasting and smelling of kerosene.

Sunset that evening was transformed by clouds gathering on the horizon, an event so rare that all work was stopped. As the orb slipped behind the cloud, a silent symphony of colors lit up the sky, and drew appreciative murmurs from them all. Jake watched the others as much as the sky itself and wondered at a people who could stop and share in the beauty of something that for himself had so often gone unnoticed.

When the spectacle finally dimmed, Jake asked through Jasmyn, "Does it ever rain here?"

"Oh yes," Omar replied. "I remember it well. It turned the plain we were walking into a river and swept away several of the animals. Then the next day the entire desert bloomed. I will never forget that vision. Good and bad together."

"When was that?"

The entire group entered into a spirited discussion. Jake waited and watched, wondering if perhaps he had broken some desert etiquette. The argument continued on until night veiled the camp and the tribe was called for the evening meal. Jake followed Jasmyn toward the cooking fire and, when they were apart from the others, asked, "Did I say something wrong?"

She looked at him with genuine surprise. "What could be wrong in asking an honest question?"

"Never mind. Come on, I want to speak with you and Pierre."

Together they walked over to where Pierre sat brooding over the sleeping form of his brother. He lifted his head at Jake's approach and declared, "We no longer have any choice, my friend."

Jake squatted down beside him. "He's worse?"

Pierre nodded, his face deeply furrowed. "I am greatly troubled. We must get him to a facility that can offer proper medical care."

"Do not trouble yourself so, mon frere," said a weak voice. All eyes turned toward Patrique. He smiled faintly and went on, "Pierre always did the worrying for both of us."

Jake asked, "How do you feel?"

"That I have more than enough strength for the task at hand," Patrique replied. "It is a good plan."

"I think so too," Jasmyn agreed.

"For myself, I am too worried to think," Pierre said. "So I must trust in the judgment of you three. Though I confess it tears at my heart to do so."

Jasmyn reached over and took his hand, her gaze as soft as her touch. "It is only for a short while, my beloved. We have been separated before, and for much longer, and much farther apart in spirit. This shall pass in the blink of an eye."

"Even that is far too long," Pierre replied.

Jake cleared his throat, the night filled by the love that spilled out from them. "You two need a couple of nights off. I'll stand watch with our friend Patrique here until we arrive in Raggah."

"They were right in what they have told me," Patrique said. "You are indeed a good friend."

Pierre looked torn. "You are sure—"

"Thank you, Jake," Jasmyn said, rising to her feet and drawing Pierre up with her.

But before they could depart, Omar walked over with two of the elders. He spoke briefly to Jasmyn, who turned and said to Jake, "Twenty-four years."

"What?"

"You asked when it had last rained. It was twenty-four years ago. They are sure."

Jake struggled to his feet. "They've spent all this time trying to figure out when it rained?"

"Smile and nod your gratitude," Jasmyn said quietly. When Jake had done so, she went on, "You are an honored guest. You asked a question, and they wished to answer you honestly. It was not a simple matter. You see, Jake, there are no calendars here, no birthdays beyond the one marking a child as an adult. Time is measured by events. They had to tie the rainfall to the events of that period, measuring back by other events. This camel had foaled, that person was born, another died, counting back over the seasons until the date was arrived at. Twenty-four years ago it rained."

"Please thank them," Jake said feebly. His mind rang with the impact of foreignness. The desert way.

Jasmyn turned and bowed and spoke solemnly. The men responded with beams of real pride. Omar patted Jake on the shoulder, turned, and walked away.

Chapter Eight

Although Patrique had a restful night, Jake found himself sleeping with one eye and ear open. So it was that he was up and ready before the guard came within ten paces. He slipped on his boots, grabbed his rifle, stood, and bent over to check on the sick man one last time. Then he heard the whispered words, "Take me with you."

He jerked. "I thought you were asleep."

"I sleep far too much. It comes and goes like the wind. You're going out on watch, yes? I want to come with you."

"I'm not sure—"

"Please, my friend. Let me share your sunrise."

Jake helped him rise and dress, then with one hand holding his rifle and the other steadying Patrique, they made their way out of camp. Awkwardly they climbed a nearby rise. When Jake had settled Patrique near the peak, he descended to the camp and returned with two glasses and the pot of watch tea. They sat and sipped in silence for a time until Patrique spoke. "I have seen you walk out while the camp was still sleeping and seen you return after the sunrise. Your face changes while you are away."

Jake hid his embarrassment behind noisy sips of his tea that cooled the liquid as he swallowed. "You've been watching me?"

"Not intentionally. But I often find it hardest to sleep around dawn." Patrique paused to sip from his own glass. "Pierre has told me of your faith. I hear in his voice how it has given him strength. But I *see* it most clearly in your face, when you return from watching the sunrise."

Patrique lifted his gaze toward the star-flecked heavens. "There were times of great despair in that dungeon, Jake. I felt as though the darkness would crush my very soul. That day, when I heard a voice call out my name, I thought at first it was death come for me. I thought the tragedy of my imprisonment had given me the power to hear what should always remain hidden."

Jake sipped quietly and shivered from more than just the night's lingering chill.

"But the voice came from above," Patrique went on. "From the only place where light entered into my dark hole. And then I knew. I was hearing an angel. An angel with the voice of my brother. Even after I knew it was real, and my nightmare might indeed come to an end, still I knew that the angels had been at work. I knew that it would take the power of heaven to pierce the darkness that enslaved me with chains upon my heart as well as my limbs. So I was not surprised when Pierre began speaking of this new power in his life. I had already seen it at work, you see. I had already sensed this power at work."

He turned to look at Jake. "So tell me, friend of my brother. What is carried upon the sunrise that leaves you with the power shining from your face?"

"I couldn't put it into words," Jake replied, ashamed by his inadequacy.

"Then show me," Patrique quietly implored. "Please."

Jake nodded once, closed his eyes in a moment's prayer, then turned his face toward the awakening east. Patrique followed his example, sitting in utter silence there beside him, his eyes searching in the gradually strengthening light for that which remained unseen.

Little by little the silence drew into their souls, stilling their mind, opening them to the quietest of sounds. Breaths of dawn wind puffed about them, whispering gentle secrets. Sand shifted and cascaded, an animal bleated, a loose fold on one of the tents flapped open and closed. The light strengthened, and with it the sense of sharing more than that which was seen with the eyes. The veil of night lifted enough to reveal an ocean of softly undulating sand waves stretching into the horizon. All was still and silent and timeless.

Jake reached into his pocket for his Bible, found his place, and read the next verse from John's gospel, "Verily, verily, I say unto you, Whosoever committeth sin is the slave of sin. And the slave abideth not in the house for ever: but the Son abideth ever. If the Son therefore shall make you free, ye shall be free indeed."

He stopped, lifted his gaze, and heard Patrique murmur to the horizon, "Free."

Jake reached over, clasped Patrique's shoulder, bowed his head, and spoke the words resounding through his silent mind and heart.

Chapter Nine

Two days later they arrived at the oasis of Raggah, a broad lake sheltered by a veritable forest of palms. When he crested the final rise and the lake came into view, Jake stopped and gaped with the others, mesmerized by the sight. In the space of three weeks, he had forgotten how beautiful so much water could be.

Swaths of green stretched down two neighboring gullies, marking the track of streams that broke through the rock and delivered their precious load overland. Amidst the trees and brush raced a wealth of wildlife—ostriches, hyenas, gazelles, monkeys. Butterflies by the millions scoured the lake's surface, feeding upon the water flowers and the blooming reeds that lined one bank. After days in the barren sand, Jake had difficulty taking in this sudden wealth of life.

Across the lake from them rose a city as yellow as the barren earth that surrounded it. The Atlas Mountains rose majestic and ocher in the background. This was the first real town Jake had seen in what felt like a lifetime. Jake was not sure he liked it. He was amazed by how his perspective had changed. When he had first left the city for the desert, he had felt he was leaving all civilization behind. Now, as he left the desert for the city, he felt as though the joys of living were soon to be lost, the beauty of life recaged, and his world filled with meaningless clamor.

Omar and Jasmyn climbed the rise to stand behind him. "Raggah is a place of great glory," Omar said, looking out over the city. "And like all such places, a home to much tragedy. It was here that the lords of the western deserts ruled the trade routes of the northern and western Saharas. Gold, ivory, myrrh, frankincense, salt, slaves—all traders paid tribute to the rulers of Raggah."

He pointed out over the cloudless distance. "From that citadel they held life-and-death power over the local tribes. The chieftains were all-powerful, ruthless, and often cruel. When the great drought drove the Tuareg into this city, Raggah and the chieftains devoured their souls. Now the French have restricted their evil, but only to a point. Their cruelty is not ended, only held in check, like a vicious dog on the Frenchmen's chain. Be careful here."

"Don't worry."

Still Omar stood and gazed out over the city. "To my people I give the wisdom of the desert and the wealth of my camels. People in towns such as these live for money. That is not our way. That is the hunger that never ends, the thirst that is never quenched no matter how deeply they draw from the well. No, money is for those who have chosen to live as the blind."

Jake stood and looked out over the city and felt the words settle to the very depths of his soul.

"We hold the wealth of blood," Omar said quietly. "By this we mean the good name of our tribe. It means we treat our animals well, we pass on the tribe's wisdom and lore to our children, we show the desert hospitality to all. It is a wealth that lasts and does not blind one to the power of the day."

He turned and faced Jake square on. "I have thought long on your words of our walk together. I have decided that our two who beg to learn will go to the Christian school. They will study the knowledge of which you have spoken. They will return and teach our people the meaning of this Christian love and Christian peace."

"You do me a great honor," Jake said, humbled by the man's gift of trust. "I will hope and pray that your decision brings new and eternal wealth to your tribe."

"This also do I hope. Come," Omar said. "Let us descend and make camp."

Travel-weary caravans from a dozen different locations took rest along the lake's shoreline. As they walked the long path skirting the oasis, Omar intoned each name in turn. "They are of the Al Moyda'at. And those the M'Barek, a good people and our friends for many generations. And on the other side, the Mahmoudi. They are not to be trusted. Beyond them the Tebbeh from the reaches far to the south, here to trade their gold for salt and wares."

Each camp was carefully guarded, showing fierce hostility to most who passed or looked their way. At one camp a man strode forth, bowed and spoke and gestured for the chieftain to join him. Jake walked on with the rest of the tribe, drawing the desert hood down farther to shield his eyes, and watched as Omar respectfully declined the invitation.

They kept themselves hidden from prying eyes by making camp at the lake's far side. At dusk a pearly glow settled over the city. From the city's ancient mosque, the muezzin called the faithful to the day's final prayer.

As night gathered, fires glowed the entire length of the lake and glimmered along the distant city's walls. Their glow and the sunset burnished the lake to a coppery sheen. Fishermen glided gracefully across this brilliant surface, poling themselves in slender boats as long as the surrounding trees were tall. Jake spent the cool hour watching these fisherfolk, two polers working bow and stern, while from amidships three others fanned out nets, tossing and pulling them in with motions older than written history.

While the evening meal was being prepared, Jake and Pierre brought Omar to the lakeside, and through Jasmyn explained the plan. He heard them out in silence, then stared out over the darkening lake. Finally he said, "For several days it has been clear that your brother is not up to the journey. But I did not feel it my place to speak first."

"It's the only idea we have had," Jake said, speaking for them all. "But if you have a better one, we would like to hear it."

Omar examined him. "How can you be sure that the French are not after him as well?"

"Even if they are, it will be for Patrique and not for us," Jake replied, hoping that what he said was true.

"It is doubtful," Pierre added, "that the traitor could order a hunt for Patrique through official French channels without revealing his plot."

"We are hoping that the people who ordered us to proceed northward will be watching for anything like that," Jake explained.

Omar pondered their words long and hard before

the call came to gather for the evening meal. Rising to his feet, the chieftain said, "I can see no danger in this plan that another plan would not also contain, and I have no other idea as sound as this one. We shall think on it further this night and see what the dawn brings before deciding."

Patrique was feeling fit enough to join them for the evening meal, but his eyes glittered feverishly in the firelight. Watching him, Jake knew at some deep level that tonight marked an ending. Come what may, this portion of his journey and his life was over. Jake looked about the campfire, studying each of the faces he had come to know so well, trying to etch the power of the memory and his feelings upon his very soul.

He sat and ate as the others did, dipping into the communal pot using only his right hand, the action totally natural now. He accepted a goatskin, drank, passed it on. He listened to words he could not understand, seated in the dust at the very frontier of civilization, surrounded by men and women who could neither read nor write, and felt himself to be the richest man on earth.

Abruptly Pierre stood, helped Jasmyn to her feet, and motioned for Jake to join them. He raised his hands for silence, then said through her, "I have told this to Omar, but I wish to also speak these words to all the tribe. It is only because of the help you have given that my brother is here and alive today. The tribe of Al-Masoud has placed upon me a debt that can never be repaid."

"Hear, hear," Patrique said hoarsely.

"Although much of my time and energy has gone to caring for my brother, still I have learned much from my time with you," Pierre went on. "One such lesson is that questions are rarely asked about what is considered private or personal. Still, I think you may like to hear how we came to be with you."

An appreciative murmur rose around the fire. Pierre looked at Jake and asked, "Shall you start, or shall I?"

"You're doing fine so far."

Pierre began with the cries of the young Lilliana Goss through the wires of the detention camp—in mistaking Pierre for his missing twin Patrique, she had set the whole saga in motion. Pierre carried them through the search for his brother in Marseille, took them along on the hot, dusty train ride to Madrid and Gibraltar, then told how Jake had saved his life both in a smugglers' cafe and again on a boulevard in Gibraltar.

The tribesmen showed themselves to be a marvelous audience. They drank in the story with the rapt attention of a people raised on stories, a folk bereft of books and film or any entertainment save what they made for themselves.

Pierre, too, became caught up in the telling, filling the spaces created by Jasmyn's translations by using his wiry body and expressive face to describe the things of which he spoke. Quietly Jake lowered himself down on his haunches so that he too could enjoy watching his friend act out the spectacle of two terrified assassins tied to hospital beds in a Gibraltar cave, with great Barbary apes glowering and screaming down at them. Jake took great pleasure in joining their delighted roar of approval.

But the desert people's strongest reactions were saved for the scenes that took place in Telouet, for here was a place they knew. When Pierre threw himself into a parody of Jake's saluting the diminutive official Hareesh Yohari, the entire camp howled. They silenced only long enough to hear of how Jasmyn had directed the search to the palace dungeon. But when Patrique stood on shaky legs to display the festering scars remaining on his wrists and ankles from the dungeon's chains, they roared like a pack of hungry lions. All had seen or heard of Patrique's injuries by then, yet now the story lived for them.

Pierre next described Jake's attempt to pull out the dungeon's window bars by means of ropes attached to the sultan's antique Rolls Royce. At that point, one of the elders became so excited that he sprang to his feet, grasped Pierre's robes, and began shaking the grinning Frenchman back and forth, jabbering at the top of his voice.

Omar himself had to stand and lead the old man back to his place before Pierre could describe the grand finale, which occurred when Jake finally lost his temper and crashed the car into the palace walls. The image of him throwing caution and silence to the wind and using a Rolls Royce as a battering ram against the palace wall had the audience rolling about the fire in helpless convulsions. And they laughed even harder at the notion of hundreds of sleepy traders being transformed into pole vaulters and high divers as a car suddenly flew down an otherwise empty street, before the sultan's own guards saluted Jake and Pierre as they drove through the gates and off to freedom and safety.

Jake watched the people gathered about the fire, saw the hands raise to wipe tears from leathery faces, and knew an astonishing pleasure. With the sharing of their tale, they had entered into the tribe's living history. He stood with the others, content beyond measure that they would now remain long after their paths and their duties had taken them elsewhere.

Chapter Ten

They came in silence and in stealth, just after dawn. They chose their moment well, arriving when the camels were being inspected. This was a normal procedure at every longer halt and was a monstrously noisy affair. Whether unloading or loading, feeding or watering, rising to their feet or lowering to their knees, sick or healthy, camels responded to every command with great complaining bellows. In the desert stillness, their bellows were audible for more than two miles. Here in the confines of the caravansary, their noise was deafening.

Jake followed Omar along his slow inspection, watching him give each hoof a careful examination, then talk long and seriously with the tribe's chief drover. They were alone. The rest of the tribe had placed as much distance as possible between them and the camels' cacophony. Occasionally Omar turned and showed something to Jake, but not often. The issues were too technical to be communicated well with hands alone. Jasmyn was busy elsewhere, fashioning Pierre's uniform to Patrique's more slender frame—an important part of their plan. Jake did not mind. Not even the camels could disturb his pleasure at walking and watching and learning.

The Tuareg's arrival caught them all by surprise. One moment, Jake was watching Omar kneel and use his knife to inspect a sensitive swelling on one hoof, while the camel punctuated their work with aggrieved bellows. The next, another knife suddenly jabbed toward Jake's ribs.

Jake's war-honed reactions took instant control. In one lightning motion he spun and grabbed and wrenched forward. Jake's lack of hesitation caught the mercenary by surprise; the Arab was pulled forward and off balance enough for Jake to force the dagger from his grip, sweep one leg out to trip him, and strike the base of his skull with a iron-hard fist.

Jake spun about in time to see Omar leap backward, avoiding the knife thrust of another Tuareg. Omar's hands were empty, his own knife lost somewhere in the dust kicked up by their struggle and the frightened animals. The drover was rolling in the dirt, fighting a third Tuareg while the camels bellowed and danced to avoid stepping on the fighting men. The remainder of the camp was blocked from view by the milling animals and the dust.

"Omar!" As he shouted, Jake tossed the knife he found in the dust at his feet. Omar flashed a swift glance, caught the knife by its haft, blocked the next parry, and shouted something back. Jake caught the tone of warning and spun in time to meet the attack of a fourth Tuareg.

The mercenary snarled a curse as Jake slithered out of the blade's reach and drew his own dagger. The hook-nosed Arab crouched and weaved, the dagger blade before him. Jake willed himself to watch the eyes and not the blade, for it was there that the first signal would come. The mercenary was skilled, however, and used his polished blade to flicker sunlight into Jake's eyes. Jake blinked at the blinding brilliance, saw the Tuareg ready for the pounce, and knew a heartbeat's quavering that he faced a more experienced foe.

Then the camel came to his rescue.

Clearly the animal had endured all the jostling it was willing to take for one day. Whether it was because the Tuareg was a stranger, or simply because he was within closest reach, the camel reached down and gripped the Tuareg's shoulder with its great yellow teeth.

The man howled, dropped his weapon, and struggled to free himself. The camel responded by lifting the man clear of the earth.

Jake sheathed his dagger, stepped forward, and put every ounce of energy he had into one solid blow to the Tuareg's midsection. The camel obliged by choosing the next moment to unceremoniously drop its cargo. Before the Arab could fold, Jake planted both feet in the prescribed manner and hammered a right to the Tuareg's chin. He felt the impact all the way down to his toes. The Tuareg lifted clear of the earth a second time before collapsing in a defeated heap.

Omar shouted a second time. Jake spun, saw that the chieftain was busy tying up his defeated foe. Omar tossed a rope and pointed back to where Jake's first attacker was stirring. Swiftly Jake knelt and bound the man's hands and feet, dragged him over, and tied him and the second Tuareg back to back. The drover hauled his own unconscious adversary over and attached him to the others, as did Omar with the fourth man. Cloths were stuffed in each mouth and the ropes were carefully checked. Omar motioned that the attackers should be left where they sprawled, blocked from view by the animals, until the remainder of the camp had been patrolled. He ordered the drover to stand guard over them, then led Jake back toward the camp.

They skirted the animal paddocks, and the tents came into view beyond a sheaf of towering palms. Something caught Omar's eye. He held up one hand, searched, then crouched and drew Jake down with him. His hand signals were so complex Jake did not understand at first. Again the hands rose to fix an imaginary cap upon his head, then down to straighten an invisible tie. Jake nodded. He was to go put on his uniform. Something was bringing the plan into action long before they had expected.

Jake skirted the outer tents, dropped to his knees at the back of his own, saw Omar rise and carefully dust himself off and straighten his clothes, then march solemnly forward, every inch the tribal chieftain. Jake lifted the back flap and rolled into the tent.

He dragged out his satchel from the tent's back corner, dug down and extracted his uniform. His actions speeded by the rise and fall of voices outside, he undressed and dressed. The uniform was heavily creased from weeks of heat and hard travel, but there was nothing he could do about that. He wiped the dust from his boots, opened the satchel's side pocket and extracted his papers, straightened his jacket, set his cap at the proper angle, then hesitated. He reached down and slid the tribal dagger into his belt, and walked from the tent.

And faltered.

He could not help it. There before him stood a sudden mystery, a Pierre shrunk and yet still the same, a

Pierre made fragile by the fever that glittered in his eyes. Jake forced himself forward, nodded at Patrique standing there in Pierre's uniform, and asked as calmly as he could, "What's going on?"

Patrique gestured toward the official standing before him. "This gentleman is here on behalf of the sultan of Raggah," he replied, and Jake could see that he was holding himself erect and calm only with the greatest effort. "They have received word that the Al-Masoud tribe was harboring two thieves. Foreigners."

Jake turned toward the slender man with swarthy skin and darting eyes. His robes were rich, his cloth-topped boots long and curled and decked with silver threads. He also appeared very nervous. Clearly, the situation here in the camp was not at all as he had expected.

Jasmyn stood at his side, quietly translating everything that was said. Jake strived to hide his surprise at her appearance; even though they had discussed it, still it was a shock to see her in a long beige skirt, pumps, blouse, and headkerchief—the only Western clothes she had carried with her. As calmly as he could, Jake shook his head and replied, "Not here. The only foreigners traveling with this tribe were us."

The official spoke, his voice very high and nasal. Jake found himself relaxing. It was hard to be afraid of somebody who sounded as if he were still on the wrong side of puberty. Jasmyn translated, "The official wishes to examine both your papers."

Together they unbuttoned their shirt pockets and proffered their passes. Jasmyn pointed to each line in turn, patiently translated everything that was written there. The official made a pretense of listening, yet all the while his eyes nervously scanned the camp. The trio of swarthy guards flanking the official were equally puzzled and far less secretive in their search of the perimeter. Jake kept his face set but thought to himself, sorry, chumps, your buddies aren't going to make this party.

The official persisted with his charade of questions about who they were, where they had come from, what they were doing with the tribe, how Jasmyn had come to be their official interpreter, and so on, and so forth. But clearly his instructions had included nothing about arresting two Allied officers in uniform, their chests decorated with medals, and their papers all in order.

Reluctantly he handed back Patrique's papers, and Jake permitted himself a full breath. Home free. For the moment.

The official turned to Jake, who already had his hand outstretched, his palm itching, then stopped. A sly glint appeared in the prince's eyes, and Jake felt the band tighten around his chest. The official withdrew the hand holding Jake's papers and spoke again in that high nasal voice. Jasmyn said, "He does not think the sultan has ever had the honor of meeting an American officer before. He wishes to invite you to the palace, where the sultan himself will return your documents and perhaps entertain you for tea."

"What can we do to stop him?"

"Nothing," she said, her melodious voice urging Jake to remain calm. "He is being an Arab, nothing more. He wishes to have the final word and show that he, too, has power."

The prince saw the spark in Jake's eyes and smiled like a well-fed cat. He spoke again, vastly pleased to have this final moment of control. Jasmyn said, "The sultan will be delighted to see you anytime tomorrow afternoon."

Jake yearned to reach over and throttle the whining little voice right out of the prince's head. All he said was, "I'll be there."

Omar stood and watched until the official was out of sight, then said through Jasmyn, "Our choices have just been taken from our grasp. We must take the injured one to safety and then, papers or no, move to safety ourselves." He looked first at Jake, then the others. "You are ready?"

Pierre stepped forward, still dressed in his desert garb. "What happened?"

Swiftly Jake recounted their attack in the camel paddock. "They planned it well. They waited until we were split off from the main camp and attacked only with knives. Swift and silent and almost deadly."

"If they left any friends watching and waiting in reserve, our escape route may already be cut off," Omar pressed. "We must hurry."

Pierre squared his shoulders. "We go."

A tremor passed across Jasmyn's lovely features. She raised a hand toward Pierre, who stepped forward and took her in his arms. He lowered his face close to hers and spoke words meant only for Jasmyn. Tears gathered and cascaded down her cheek as she nodded once, raised her head, and returned a soft and lingering kiss before allowing Pierre to step back, take a shaky breath, and say, "Let us proceed while we still are able."

Chapter Eleven

There is no longer any need for subterfuge," Omar said as they walked toward Raggah, their pace set by Patrique. "As soon as we accomplish our task here, we shall leave all our tribe but a chosen few with the M'Barek tribe. They are an honorable folk and can be trusted to treat our people well. Then we shall proceed with all haste across the northern reaches for Melilla."

"If this works," Pierre said quietly.

When the translation was made, Omar shook his head. "We no longer have a choice. It must work."

Small squadrons of Omar's men flanked them as they walked. They carried their weapons with deceptive ease, sauntering along before and after the group, far enough away not to grant a threatening impression to the city's guards, yet close enough to defend at an instant's warning.

Pierre said to Jake, "I had no idea you could handle a knife."

"I can't," Jake replied. "That camel saved my bacon."

"She was merely repaying your earlier kindness," Omar said through Jasmyn.

"My what?"

"Did you not recognize her as one of those you led back to safety across the barren land?"

"They all look pretty much the same to me," Jake confessed.

"Then be thankful that the camel was more discerning," Omar replied, humor glinting in his dark eyes. "Nonetheless, I agree with you. The gift of good fortune has shone on you this morning. Let us hope it holds."

The central streets of Raggah were shaded by tall trees whose desert-trained roots reached deep enough to tap the underground water. The lanes opened into great ceremonial plazas, dusty spaces with large central wells lined by palms. All commerce took place under the trees' shade. Whole families gathered upon layers of bright desert carpets, living out their daily lives beneath the ancient trees. All conversation, all trade halted to watch the spectacle of two foreign officers in uniform and the beautiful woman in Western clothing. Only when they had passed beyond view did the desert city life resume.

Farther along, plastered alcoves had been cleverly built to melt into the line of trees, making for a covered market. Here men and women from all the tribes of northern Africa gathered to barter wares. Despite the numerous caravans camped alongside the lake, the display in the town's market was disappointing. Omar watched Jake take note of the paltry wares and through Jasmyn explained, "Here is evidence of the city's corrupt nature. Nowadays, everything of value is traded in secret. Not even the names of the traders are bandied about openly."

The houses were buttressed and fortlike, with thick clay walls and windows too narrow for even a child to crawl through. The central mosque was built like a pyramid, with precious logs used to support its five-story structure. Upon the city's sandy lanes walked wild-looking desert warriors, all armed with ancient rifles slung upside down over one shoulder and grasped by the barrels. The position of the rifles, according to Jasmyn, was a sign that they came in peace.

Water was delivered from house to house in goat-skins. There was no electricity, no lights, no advertisements, and no motor vehicles in the central city, for the prince prohibited them all. Jake found the city unnaturally still for its size, as though beaten into submission and held in quiet despair.

The French outpost came into view just in time. Patrique crossed the heat-stricken square on legs that barely had the strength to hold him aloft. His breath rasped noisily, and his features were streaked with sweat. His gaze was blank, unfocused; all his attention was drawn to the struggle of putting one foot in front of the other.

With a single word Omar stopped his men from continuing with them. Silently they slipped into neighboring shadows and vanished from sight.

The outpost stood separate and isolated from its neighboring structures, with the only raised wooden porch Jake had seen in the entire city. A pair of flags hung limply in the dusty heat. A lone Arab soldier in puttees sweltered at guard duty. He eyed them with tired hostility as they approached.

As they arrived at the bottom stair, Omar gave an almost imperceptible motion to Pierre—they were to remain there. Jasmyn saw and understood, and a choked sob forced its way through her locked throat.

"No tears," Pierre murmured. "Be strong for us all,

my beloved, and look to when we will be united before everyone, for all our days."

Jasmyn lifted her chin once again, her face set with tragic determination. Without looking Pierre's way, she whispered, "My heart, my prayers, my very reason for living goes with you."

Together they climbed the stairs. On the top step, Patrique faltered and would have gone down had Jake and Jasmyn not gripped his arms and held him upright. The Arab soldier took a hesitant step forward, then turned and shouted into the dark interior.

A bored Frenchman wearing desert uniform and corporal's stripes stepped into view. His eyes widened at the sight of an unknown French officer being half carried toward him. He bolted forward, took Patrique's arm from Jasmyn, and barked something at Jake. Jasmyn replied in a hesitant tremolo, which the corporal clearly took as worry over the officer's state. Patrique moaned a brief reply of his own.

"Tell him we were traveling on official duty through the western Sahara when Major Pierre Servais was stricken with an unknown illness," Jake said, his voice officer-sharp, speaking more to establish himself as an American than because the words were important. "You, as his nurse, must immediately escort him to a military hospital."

The corporal gaped at him as together they eased Patrique down onto the barren office's only bench. Jasmyn continued to speak, her voice desolate with loss. Jake was sorry for her, but at the same time felt that her sadness was the perfect attention grabber. Nobody could have faked the concern she was showing.

"The corporal says that the nearest clinic is at the

Foreign Legion fortress in Colombe-Bechar," Jasmyn said.

"How far?"

"If we leave now by transport, we could arrive before nightfall. He will have to radio and obtain permission before we can take the truck."

"Tell him to hurry," Jake said, and bent over Patrique's sweat-drenched form. "You're gonna make it, buddy. Almost home free."

"I'm so very thirsty," Patrique replied.

Jasmyn spoke with the corporal, who went to his desk, poured out the half glass remaining in his water bottle, and carried it over to Patrique. He spoke to Jasmyn, who said to Jake, "He says there is a good tearoom down the side street and across the next square. I could go—"

Jake straightened. "I'll do it."

"But Pierre—"

Jake looked at her hard and spoke very carefully, "The only way we will know if everything is all right with Patrique's being transported to the official French government hospital is if you are here to overhear whatever they say."

Her shoulders slumped in defeat. "You are right. Of course."

He patted her arm, murmured, "Be strong," and was out the door.

Jake bolted down the stairs, motioned for Omar and Pierre to follow him, and headed down the side passage. Once out of sight he said, "Patrique's losing a lot of liquid. We need to get him something to drink. Both of them, for that matter."

"And the plan?"

"Looks like the soldier's bought it. He's radioing for

permission to drive him to the hospital at someplace called Colombe-Bechar."

"Colombe-Bechar," Omar repeated, using the Arab pronunciation, then nodding his head vigorously. The destination clearly met with his approval.

The tea house's interior was as grand as the exterior was simple. Arched colonnades gave the great hall a pretense of being separated into a series of interconnected chambers. The pillars were of darker granite, the floor of polished marble slabs, the walls of grand desert carpets and ornate mosaic designs. The sound of dice and slapped backgammon chips accented the lively talk. Hookahs bubbled and sent up pungent clouds of smoke. A central fountain tinkled merrily, spraying out a continual sheen of perfumed water.

Omar ignored the silence and the stares that their appearance caused and imperiously ordered a waiter into swift action. Within minutes a tray was brought bearing heavily sweetened tea and glasses of cooled honey and curds. Jake drained his glass in one thirsty gulp and then reached for his tea. "I want to get back and see if everything is all right."

"Agreed." Pierre licked at his white moustache and took the tray with the extra servings. He said to Omar simply, "Patrique and Jasmyn."

But when Pierre turned for the door, the waiter grasped his arm and began arguing. Omar reached into the leather purse slung from his belt and spoke soothing words. Impatiently Jake stepped back into the sunlight.

As he moved across the square, he felt the bottom drop from his world when a familiar voice hissed, "Yes indeedy, just as was thinking. Is the one destroying Hareesh Yohari's world and home and life."

Jake spun and found himself facing a diminutive figure, hopping from one foot to the other with rage, his head raised to eye level by standing on the well's stone border, both hands gripping an ancient single-shot pistol. From Jake's perspective, the gun looked as big as a cannon. All he could think to say was, "How's business?"

"Business, yes, man now speaking of business. I speaking of business too. Business of missing Rolls Royce motor vehicle. Business of palace wall and escaping prisoner. Business of ruining life of sultan's official chief assistant." He shook the barrel inches from Jake's eyes. "But I am making all correct. Yes. Am bringing head of number one criminal back to sultan, sitting on front of formerly stolen Rolls Royce motor vehicle. Now you are telling me where—"

"Is that who I think it is?"

Hareesh Yohari jumped and spun about. His eyes widened at the sight of Pierre marching toward him, dressed in desert garb and burned to a leathery brown, bearing a gleaming tray with tea and curds. The little official squeaked, "You!"

Then Jake did the only thing that came to mind, which was to bend over and grip Yohari's ankles, lift, and fling the man over the lip of the well. The sultan's former official gave a lingering wail that ended with a resounding splash. Jake straightened up and did not bother to mask his grin. "All in a good day's work."

"Come, my friend," Pierre said. "The tea is growing cold."

They turned the corner to find a dusty jeep stationed in front of the French post, its motor idling noisily. "For once my army has acted with dispatch and efficiency," Pierre proclaimed. "I must write a note of commendation once I am again myself."

Jasmyn appeared at the head of the stairs, Patrique leaning heavily upon her. Her eyes fastened upon Pierre and remained so throughout the maneuver of loading the sick man into the jeep. Yet she said nothing. Her gaze shifted only when the corporal came around the jeep and officiously helped her in. She permitted the man to load her into the back beside Patrique, shook her head to the proffered tea, and handed both glasses to Patrique, who drank greedily. Then her eyes turned to Jake. "Colonel Burnes."

"Yes, ma'am."

"You are to take care of my treasure," she said quietly, her gaze dark with unspoken loss.

"With my life." Jake fumbled over the affection he felt for that beautiful, brave woman. "Everything I've learned here has been because of you."

"No, Colonel," she corrected. "I have helped. But you have learned because you have wanted to. You have not been stopped by the alien surroundings or the hardship or the fatigue. You have given great honor to my mother's people. I am proud of you. As are they."

"Jake," Patrique called hoarsely. "Thank you."

Before Jake could reply, the corporal gunned the motor and wheeled the jeep in a tight circle. Through the rising dust Jasmyn looked back at Pierre, and as a single tear escaped she mouthed the words, *I love you.*

Then she was gone.

Chapter Twelve

J ake followed Omar back to where the tribesmen waited, giving Pierre silent space to compose himself and erase the naked emotions that lay etched upon his features. Already he felt Jasmyn's absence, and not just because of his friend's sorrow. There was a new barrier between Omar and him, one that respect and hand signals could never fully cancel.

Behind them, a hysterical voice began shouting incomprehensible words. They spun about, and spotted a wet and bedraggled Hareesh Yohari emerge from the side passage and limp furiously across the square toward them.

Pierre mused aloud, "Now how did he get out of that well so swiftly?"

A band of desert warriors appeared from the shadows behind Yohari. At the sight of Omar they howled their fury. Omar hissed, "Tuareg."

"That explains it," Jake said.

Omar pressed them forward and ordered his tribesmen into a phalanx blocking the alcove behind them. They turned and fled as the passage erupted into fighting, shouting men.

Omar led them in a twisting, winding pattern

down countless, nameless streets. From time to time they would catch wind of voices shouting and calling to unseen fellows, before Omar jinked and sped them off in a different direction.

The chase forced them farther and farther away from the oasis and the tribe and safety. Every time Omar sought to direct them around and back toward the camp, voices barely one street over warned them away.

Jake crouched with the others in a shallow doorway, panting and sweating and feeling like a prey hunted by beaters, driven toward exposure and death.

He opened his mouth to tell Pierre that it was time to separate, to let him and Omar try to draw them off while Pierre escaped with Patrique's testimony on the traitor. He knew it was futile, that his friend would never let others sacrifice themselves so that he could live, yet all the same he had to at least try.

Suddenly the voices of the approaching mercenaries were drowned out by a sound once familiar to Jake, and yet now so alien that for a moment he thought it was thunder.

He craned and searched the empty spaces overhead, when abruptly the sun was blocked from view by a great roaring beast. Before the sky again emptied, Jake was up and racing and shouting behind him, "Come on!"

They sprinted with all the strength they had left, Omar following a pace behind them and shouting fearful words they could neither understand nor spare breath to answer. Jake followed the sound of revving motors out beyond the final border of houses, through the great sand-and-mortar embankment erected as the city's first line of defense, over the first line of dunes, up the second, where he flattened himself into a shallow crevice and drew the others down with a swift motion of his hand.

Cautiously they raised their heads over the summit and looked down at a long, flat stretch of rocky terrain marked only by a series of blackened oil barrels, a dusty shed of corrugated sheeting, and a limp French flag. They scarcely saw any of it. Their attention remained fastened upon the behemoth standing just beneath their perch. Its four great engines idled noisily, impatient to break free from its earthly bonds and fling heavenward once more.

The Lancashire bomber had seen many hundreds of hours of hard wartime service. Bullet holes traced a silvered pattern from wing to tail, the flaps were streaked with oil and ancient grime, one side window was starred and shattered, and two of the wheels were worn down to dangerous white patches. Despite all this, the great plane bore its age and scars with pride, and the engines rumbled with smooth accuracy. It was the sweetest sound Jake had ever heard.

"Beautiful," Pierre murmured, clearly agreeing with him.

The pilot clattered down the back loading ramp, pushing an overloaded trolley and carrying a folded sheaf of papers in his mouth. Behind him came a single Arab guard, pushing a second trolley piled so high with boxes that he had to crane around the side to find his footing. Together they maneuvered their cargo into the rusting warehouse.

"Now's as good as it's going to get," Jake whispered.

Omar hissed, causing them to swivel about on their bellies. A cadre of Tuareg appeared in the embankment's narrow opening, searching the empty desert reaches and arguing fiercely among themselves.

Keeping himself below the lip of the defile, Jake slid the knife from his belt and offered it back to Omar. "I wish you could know what it has meant to travel with you," he whispered.

Omar looked down at the knife for a very long moment, then pushed it back toward Jake.

"I can't," Jake murmured, reaching out once more.

Again Omar pressed the hand back, harder this time, and pointed with his chin toward the waiting plane. Go.

Jake grasped the chieftain's shoulder and held it firmly. Omar returned the gaze and nodded once. He understood.

Pierre reached over and gripped the chieftain's hand. "I owe you much," he whispered. "I will repay. A way will be found."

Omar murmured a reply, the meaning clear.

Jake slithered forward and rolled over the edge, followed by Pierre. Together they scrambled down the dune, raced at a crouch across the open terrain, and pounded up the plane's loading ramp.

Inside, the noise was deafening. The plane's age was visible everywhere, from the rusting struts to the string of bullet holes that provided the interior's only light and ventilation. The hold was mammoth and filthy and rocked continually in time to the droning engines. Boxes and bales were strapped along both sides, and loose padding littered the central gangway.

Jake was still standing there, trying to get his bearings, when voices approached and shouted words indistinguishable over the engines' roar. Panicked into action, he and Pierre ripped up padding, pressed themselves into two empty pockets between the bundled cargo, crouched down, and flung the filthy burlap over their heads.

A pair of boots climbed the metal ramp, shouted something more, then operated a winch that ground and groaned and finally pulled the ramp up tight with a resounding bang. The boots walked forward, passed Jake's hiding place, and headed up into the cockpit.

The engines' roar rose to a new pitch. The plane rattled and groaned and trundled slowly about. The thunder rose even higher, the ground bumped beneath them, then with a gut-wrenching swoop they felt themselves leap from the earth.

Jake eased himself as much as he could in his cramped position and took a couple of easier breaths. Safe.

Then he almost jumped out of his skin when a voice shouted just inches from his ear, "Well if this ain't a sight for sore eyes, I don't know what is."

A boot kicked at his shin, and the Texas twang went on, "You two come on outta there. My copilot's down with the galloping whatsis, and this baby don't fly too well without a firm hand on the tiller."

Chapter Thirteen

L ucky for you boys I was blocking the guardhouse window," the pilot told them once they had joined him in the cockpit. "That Arab back there woulda probably shot you for renegades. Me, now, I got a naturally curious nature. I see what appears to be an American Army officer skedaddling for my plane with an Arab in them fancy desert robes hot on his tail, why, I figure this is probably one for the books."

He pointed through his window and went on, "That river coming out of the Raggah oasis used to be almost two miles wide. Now it's not much more than a stream. Not much farther on, it just gets swallowed up by the desert. This lake here is the last gathering place for waters that used to be wide as an inland sea."

Jake tried to match his easy tone. "How do you know all this?"

"Oh, you mosey around these parts long enough, you'd be surprised what you learn. So happens I like the desert and the people. Folks around here haven't bothered with the folderol of people back home. Got a lot to teach us, if only we'd unplug our ears and stop thinking of them as backward. They're perfectly adapted to where they live. Why, you put one of your so-called civilized fellas down here, and they wouldn't last a week."

The pilot eyed Jake. "Which brings me to ask what you're doing here."

"I can't tell you."

"Like that, is it. Well, long as it's not breaking the laws of here or home, I'm not bothered."

"It's perfectly legal," Jake said. "Sort of."

"Sounds like a good desert-type answer to me." He gave them both another up-and-down inspection. "You don't aim on skinning me while I'm driving this crate, are you? So happens I'm right partial to living."

Out of the corner of his eye Jake spotted a worn and tattered Bible crammed in with flight documents. He plucked it out, held it before him, and said, "I give you my word as a Christian that I mean you no harm."

"Well, I guess that's good enough for me." He stuck out a leathery hand. "Frank Towers. Formerly of the United States Army Air Force, currently head of Tower Transport, the only asset of which you're crouching in."

"Jake Burnes. Commander of the garrison at Karlsruhe. And this is Major Pierre Servais, head of the French base at Badenburg."

That brought a start. "You're a Frenchie?"

"I am indeed," Pierre replied, extending his own hand. "I am happy to meet you, Mr. Towers."

"Likewise. You boys musta been out there quite a while, to get as sunburned and sandblasted as you look."

"Quite a while," Jake agreed solemnly.

"Why don't you slide yourself on into the copilot's chair, Colonel. You'd be a durn sight more comfortable, and I won't have to keep craning around to see you."

"Thanks. The name is Jake."

"Pull down that seat in the bulkhead there beside you, Major."

"Pierre."

"Right you are. It'll take both hands, seeing as how it ain't been used since the war. Can't afford a radio man, and even if I could, most of the places I fly don't have a soul on the air I could talk to."

"What are you doing here, if you don't mind my asking?" Jake said.

"A likely question. Joined up in thirty-nine, flew them lend-lease planes 'til we decided to jump into the fighting ourselves. After that, well, I flew just about anything you'd care to name." He eyed Jake in the seat beside him. "That true, what you said about being a Christian?"

"It is."

"This I can confirm," Pierre said gravely. "My friend has taught me not only with words, but with the way he tries to live."

"That's nice. Real nice. Myself, I saw the light after getting shot down around Arnheim. Guess maybe you heard about that. Brother, let me tell you, that was one whale of a mess. Anyway, I managed to crawl back to where it was safe, but I lost a lot of good buddies out there. So I started looking for answers, something that'd make some sense of what I'd been going through." He pointed at the Book in Jake's hand. "Had a buddy start showing me things in there, stuff I'd heard all my life but never bothered to think about before. Been trying to live up to the Master's example ever since."

Frank Towers stretched out his lanky frame as much as the cramped cockpit would allow. "After the fighting was over, I didn't have much to go home to. Then this mission group came by the church I was attending at our air base in England, said they were planting some schools down here and asked if maybe I'd fly out supplies. Craziest thing I ever heard of, but somehow I sorta felt like I was being called to help out. One thing led to another, and now all of a sudden I've got a name down here. Got more and more folks coming by, asking me to take this and that to places I never even heard of before, can't hardly find them on the map first time out."

He gave an expansive grin. "Things've gotten so busy I'm about ready to buy my second plane. Don't suppose either of you boys knows how to fly a crate?"

"Not a chance," Jake said.

"Sorry," Pierre replied.

"No matter. There's a lot of fly-boys out there looking for something that'll keep 'em in the air. It'd be nice to find another believer, though."

Jake swiveled in his seat and gave Pierre a long hard look. The Frenchman's features screwed up momentarily before he nodded slowly.

Jake turned back and said, "Seems to me we should trust you with our story."

"Well, now, there ain't nothing I like much better than a good yarn. 'Specially when we got a full day of flying stretching out in front of us."

"A day?" Pierre exclaimed.

"Where are we going?" Jake asked.

"Oh, guess I didn't tell you." The wide-mouth grin reappeared. "Either of you boys ever had any thought of visiting Malta?"

Chapter Fourteen

L et me see if I got this straight," Frank Towers said, sipping cold coffee with one hand while the other guided their thundering craft over sparkling blue Mediterranean waters. "You're aiming on stepping off this plane and going straight to the British authorities—"

"Or whatever authorities are in charge," Jake corrected.

"Son, the only folks in charge on Malta are the British, and they ain't near as much in charge as they'd like. But let's leave that for a while." He was enjoying himself immensely. "So you aim on marching straight up to the chief honcho himself and apologizing on account of the fact that one set of papers are traveling across the Sahara with the wrong fella, namely the major's very own long-lost twin brother, who just happens to be wearing his uniform. Meanwhile, the colonel's ID is in some backwater sultan's rear pocket. Then you're gonna spin this tale about an admiral perched at the other end of the Med who thinks you're the cat's pajamas and how you need to borrow one of his boats so you can get to France and save the country."

Slowly Frank shook his head. "Man, are you ever in for a shock."

"It's not a tale," Jake insisted. "It's the truth. All of it."

"Oh, I believe you. Trouble is, I doubt if you'd get past the corporal of the guard without papers, and sure as granny's lost spectacles he ain't gonna risk his stripes on any yarn like that one."

Pierre leaned forward and said, "Enlighten us."

"Right. To begin with, Malta was hit sixteen ways from Sunday in the war. The island's been a British enclave for a donkey's years, and they were using it as the main supply point for the desert war, and then for the invasion of Italy. Perfect place for a supply point, let me tell you. That's why I've set up there. It's the closest you can come to North Africa and still find a taste of home. So where was I?"

"The war," Jake said, staring out the window. Sparkling sunlit water stretched out in every direction as far as he could see. It was breathtakingly beautiful, and yet he could not help but feel as though it did not belong. So much water.

"Right. The Germans bombed it with everything they had, and the Maltese put up with it. They're a tough bunch. Scrappy. They like the British, and they hated the Germans, but now that the war's over, they want to be repaid for all they did by getting their independence. And the British, bless their souls, they'd probably give it to them, give or take another coupla hundred years. Only the Maltese figure they've earned the right to rule themselves now. And they're getting jumpy, if you know what I mean. So here you've got an important naval depot, hundreds of ships, a city that's gone through years of bombing, and people that're fast running out of patience."

"Confusion," Pierre offered. "Chaos."

"You said it. Whole island reminds me of the time a squirrel crawled up the leg of my daddy's overalls."

Malta was a rocky jewel set in the glittering azure of the Mediterranean. The capital, Valletta, was a hodgepodge of structures and styles. Steep-sided hills rising from the water were crammed with buildings from many different eras. A number were in ruins.

"Seems like everybody's conquered Malta at one time or another," Frank Towers told them. "Romans, Greeks, Arabs, Turks, French, British, Italians, even the Holy Roman Empire. Every one of 'em's ended up cussing at the Maltese people's stubbornness and their clannishness. They're proud, these people. Reminds me of folks back home. But their islands were too small to build up a strong army. So they've had to put up with more than their share of foreign tyrants."

Valletta was dominated by the Grand Harbor, and the harbor by a large central spit of land, and the spit by an ancient fortress—or more accurately, a dozen fortresses built like crumbling steps one upon the other. From the air, much of the capital looked the same, with houses and official buildings alike erected upon the ruins of other, older structures.

When Jake commented on that, Towers replied, "I heard a tale the first time I touched down here. Back before the war a Roman bath was discovered directly under Valletta's central fish market. It was so well preserved that archaeologists flocked here from all over the world. Trouble was, these experts found themselves working in a steady rain of fish scales and rotting garbage, on account of the Maltese absolutely refused to move their fish market someplace else. Why should they? Another conqueror, more ruins, who cared?"

The Grand Harbor was a vast rock-lined sea perhaps ten miles wide and laced with numerous inlets, all filled with British ships, both merchant and navy. The waters gleamed gold and copper in the late afternoon sun. Jake said, "I don't think I've ever seen so many warships in one place before."

"This place is no stranger to men of war," the pilot agreed. "Not to war either. Like I said, the Germans bombed it almost every day for three solid years. Sometimes as many as fifty air sorties every day."

"It's a wonder anyone survived."

"You'd be surprised. Like you can see, the main town here was blasted to smithereens, a lot of it, anyway. Except the churches. They're in pretty good shape, overall. Strange how the Germans managed to shoot around the biggest buildings like that. Anyway, most of the islanders lived through it to tell the tale, hunkered down in these big ol' caves. Like I said, they're a stubborn lot, these Maltese. They just plain refused to give in. Worked like the dickens to help the Allies. The king gave them the George Cross. First time an entire people was ever granted such an honor."

They flew inland to the airfield near the village of Luqa. As they entered into their final approach, Towers had Jake and Pierre return to their hiding places in the cargo hold.

They landed with a thud and rolled across an uneven surface. As the brakes squealed and the engines drummed to a halt, Jake bundled the burlap wrapping up and around him. The air ached in the sudden silence.

"Not a peep from either one of you," Towers warned, passing down the hold's central gangway. "I'll be back as soon as I can. If you hear voices, play dead."

The winch creaked noisily as the rear loading platform was lowered. A fresh breeze blew through the hold. Through the burlap Jake smelled fragrances he seemed to recall from another lifetime—flowers, pine, ripening earth, a hint of the sea.

The minutes stretched into endless hours, and Jake fought against the restlessness of cramped and aching muscles. He dozed for a time, jerked awake as voices came within range and then passed by, dozed again.

The light had faded and the evening breeze had turned cool by the time Frank Towers returned. "Okay," he said softly. "Coast is clear."

Jake tossed aside the burlap over his face and scratched his scalp. "What time is it?"

"Almost midnight."

Another heap of burlap groaned, shivered, and fell to reveal a vastly disgruntled Pierre. "Which day?"

"I don't think I can move," Jake said.

"Had to wait until things settled down for the night," Towers said, crouching over a canvas duffel. He pulled out two zip-up flight coveralls and tossed them toward the groaning men. "Slip these on. If anybody stops us, you're new crew I've taken on for the second plane."

With every muscle complaining, Jake stripped and dressed in the airman's one-piece uniform. He rolled up his army dress and tucked it in the canvas sack. "You really think this is necessary?"

"Hard to say. But at least this way your friends in

Gibraltar will be able to grease your slide in, if you see what I mean."

"It makes sense," Pierre agreed.

"So what now?" Jake asked.

"You two look dead on your feet," Towers replied. "Some friends of mine run a little guesthouse down the road a ways. Nothing fancy, but the food's good and the beds are clean."

"Sounds perfect," Jake said, suddenly ravenous. "But we don't have any money on us."

"Don't you worry about that just yet, I'll take care of it and you can pay me back later. We'll just get you settled in there for what's left of the night. I've got an idea of how we can move forward, but it's gonna mean an early start tomorrow." Towers grinned at Jake's almost silent moan. "Like they say, Colonel, you can sleep when the war's over."

Chapter Fifteen

They were up and out before dawn, rumbling down the steeply sloped terrain in a car that appeared to be held together with spit and baling wire. Jake's single cup of coffee before departure had barely dented his drowsiness. But five minutes into the journey he was as awake as he had ever been in his entire life.

He leaned forward and said, "Do you think maybe you could ask the driver to slow down a little?"

"Wouldn't do a bit of good," Towers replied cheerfully. "Folks around these parts say the Maltese don't drive on the left or the right, but in the shade. And they're taught to drive fast to keep up a steady breeze."

The ancient vehicle raced down the hillside so fast the dawn-tinted vista outside Jake's window was reduced to a pallid blur. Every now and then, tendrils of fog teased their way across the street, obliterating all view of what lay ahead. "How can he see where we're going?"

"Probably can't," Towers said. "But there aren't many roads on this island. He knows every twist and turn by heart."

Jake decided that watching was doing his nerves no

good whatsoever, so he turned to his friend. No help there. Pierre's face was an interesting shade of green. He turned back to the front. "How can you sit there so unconcerned?"

"Oh, I've found that driving around this island does my prayer life a powerful lot of good," Towers replied easily.

They crested a final rise, and the city of Valletta came into view. Below them stretched a web of narrow, hilly streets, running down to the Grand Harbor and the Mediterranean's glorious blue. "The city was built by the Knights of St. John after they were kicked out of the Holy Land by the Ottomans," Towers told them. "The original Knights of St. John were founded around the year eleven hundred. They were people who helped Christians visiting the Holy Land, which wasn't all that easy with the Ottomans in charge. Charles of Spain gave them the island after the Arabs finally kicked them out of Jerusalem, and they came here and built the fortress you see down there. They made Valletta the capital in 1530."

Whenever the narrow lanes reached a level patch, they opened into great stone-lined squares. Imposing churches stood surrounded by solid North Africa-type houses. Their little taxi whizzed through the empty plazas, then plunged back into rutted ways as pitched and tilting as a roller coaster track. Signs of war and ruin were everywhere.

"The knights were known as the fighting monks," Towers went on, seemingly oblivious to the taxi's death-defying speed. "Six hundred of them and four thousand locals fought and held off an invasion of thirty thousand Ottomans. But with time the knights became richer and forgot that they were supposed to be brothers to the locals and not princes. Knight-generals started trying to outshine whatever their predecessors had built, blind to everything but their own selfish desires for earthly grandeur. The islanders were forgotten, ignored, and grew poorer. The gulf widened, and so when the French came at the end of the eighteenth century, the islanders welcomed them with open arms. They remained under the French until the British took control during the Napoleonic wars."

The driver turned onto a grand boulevard lined with imposing buildings of state. "The main street of Valletta, Sta de Real," Towers said. "We're almost there now."

They turned onto another nameless alley and stopped before a tiny shop that differed from its neighbors only because the metal outer door had been drawn halfway up and because a crowned symbol over the shuttered window proclaimed that this was a local post office. Frank Towers was already out of the taxi before it had fully halted. He tapped on the door, which was opened by a sleep-touseled older gentleman. The man shook Frank's hand and motioned impatiently for Jake and Pierre to enter.

Once they had slipped into the little shop, the proprietor slid the metal portal back down. He lifted the ancient lantern and led them into the back room, then set the lantern upon a table that was bare save for an ancient telegraph set. He seated himself, coded in, waited, listened at his headset, coded again. The minutes passed in silence. Finally he straightened, looked up at Frank Towers, and nodded once.

"Okay, boys, it's all yours."

Jake looked at him. "What is?"

"You said you had buddies in Gibraltar, didn't you?

Okay, now's your chance. Only make it fast. I promised the old gent here we'd be done and gone before he opened for the day."

Jake seated himself, scrunched his head in concentration, then requested a patch-through to the Gibraltar garrison. The minutes dragged until the code sounded. He keyed in, THIS IS COLONEL JAKE BURNES. URGENT I SPEAK IMMEDIATELY WITH COMMANDER TEAVES OR ADMIRAL BINGHAM. TOP PRIORITY.

Again there was an interminable wait. Jake turned and asked for a pad and pencil, which would make the return messages easier to read clearly. Finally the set coded back, TEAVES HERE. REQUEST CONFIRMATION OF WHO IS ON THE LINE.

Jake grinned. Commander Harry Teaves was an American Naval officer assigned garrison duty in Gibraltar, and the man who helped them during their hunt for Patrique. Jake keyed in, HELLO HARRY. HOW ARE MILLIE AND THE APES?

The response was instantaneous. JAKE, YOU OLD JOKER. KNEW YOU WERE TOO TOUGH TO HOLD DOWN. SORRY TO INFORM YOU RECEIVED REPORT OF YOUR DEMISE SOMEWHERE IN THE BACK OF BEYOND. ASSUME YOU ARE THEREFORE SPEAKING FROM HEAVEN.

Jake said to Pierre, "Somebody's claimed the reward on my head."

"It appears they try to use your papers as evidence," Pierre agreed, squinting to decipher Jake's handwriting. "Pity we must disappoint them."

Jake keyed in, YOU ARE NOT FAR OFF. AM IN MALTA.

There was a moment's pause, then, NO DOUBT A

STORY THERE BUT MUST WAIT. SERVAIS WITH YOU?

ONE OF THEM. PATRIQUE TAKEN ILL, SENT TO FRENCH GARRISON HOSPITAL COLOMBE-BE-CHAR.

SITUATION CRITICAL HERE. URGENT REPEAT URGENT WE RECEIVE INFORMATION ON POSSI-BLE TRAITOR.

Reading over his shoulder, Pierre murmured, "It appears, my friend, that your speculation was correct. The stakes were much higher than we thought."

"Shame they're playing with our lives on the table," Jake replied, and keyed in, WE CARRY WRITTEN CONFIRMATION. WHERE DO WE DELIVER?

IMPERATIVE YOU PROCEED TO US EMBASSY IN PARIS. ASK FOR WALTERS. HE IS YOUR FRIEND IN NEED. WAIT ONE. There was a long pause, then, OFFICIAL CONTACT IN MALTA QUESTIONABLE, NEW COMMANDANT, UNKNOWN TO BINGHAM. WE WILL MAKE SEARCH FOR ALLIES, BUT MUST MOVE WITH CAUTION. CAN YOU MAKE IT ON YOUR OWN?

PARIS. YOU DO NOT ASK MUCH, DO YOU. Jake thought a moment, then continued, PATRIQUE SER-VAIS AT HOSPITAL ACCOMPANIED BY JASMYN COLTRANE. URGENT YOU RESCUE THEM BEFORE TOO LATE.

CONSIDER IT DONE. ANYTHING ELSE?

HOW ABOUT SOME FUNDS?

TRANSFER POSSIBLE. GIVE NAME AND BANK.

Jake asked Towers, "What's your bank here?"

"Midland. Why?"

FRANK TOWERS. MIDLAND BANK. MALTA BRANCH.

WILL DO TODAY. MALTA. HOW ON EARTH?

MEET ME IN PARIS. I WILL TELL YOU ALL ABOUT IT.

ROGER THAT. WILL CONTACT WALTERS MY-SELF TODAY. ANY WAY HE CAN GET A MESSAGE BACK TO YOU?

Jake asked and received the post office's address and telegraph code. When he had passed on the information, he finished with, THANKS FOR HELPING HAND.

TOO FEW GOOD MEN AS IT IS. TAKE CARE. WATCH THE OLD NOGGIN. LET ME KNOW IF WE CAN DO MORE. WILL GET BUSY ON THIS END. SEE IF WE CAN RUSTLE UP SOME CAVALRY. TEAVES OUT.

Frank Towers inspected the page of messages over Jake's shoulder and said, "I guess you really are who you say you are."

Jake turned around. "You didn't believe us?"

"Let's just say I was keeping a healthy dose of skepticism right close at hand," Towers replied cheerfully. "There's a lot of tall-talers walking about these days, especially on the routes I'm flying. Anyway, glad I let you boys come along for the ride."

"We are too," Pierre replied. "And we are in your debt. Those are words I am saying quite often these days, but true just the same."

"Speaking of which," Jake said, "you will hopefully be receiving a hefty sum in the next few days."

"Might as well come to me," Towers drawled. "Seeing as how I aim on collecting as much as possible for services rendered."

"You mean you'll help us?" Jake asked, then added, "More than you already have, I mean?"

"I've gotten you this far, might as well see where we end up."

"That's great," Jake said with feeling. "Is there any chance I could send another message to the U.S. Embassy in Paris?"

The old gentleman spoke for the first time, in English starched by an accent Jake had never heard before. "Is unlikely they have direct line," he replied. "Leave message and I will send it myself."

"You can trust ol' Carlos," Towers assured them. "I oughta know. I'm planning on making an honest woman of his daughter."

"Right." Jake seated himself and swiftly composed a message to Consul Walters. He passed over the sheet and asked, "What now?"

"From the sounds of things, your best bet would be to lay low for a spell," Towers replied, looking a question at the old man.

Carlos thought a minute, then replied simply, "Mdina."

"Perfect," Towers said.

"What is that?"

"Old capital. Also known as Notabile. Place is pretty as a picture and about as far off the beaten track as you can get on an island this size. I've got a buddy up there. C'mon, let's go see if he can stash you in some hole for a coupla days."

Chapter Sixteen

The air was freshened by the steady sea breeze, warmed by the brilliant sun, and filled with birdsong and the fragrance of flowers. To their immense relief, Towers secured them transport with a driver willing to drive slower in return for a sizable tip. He kept his speed down, but punctuated his driving with scornful snorts for all fainthearted foreigners. Jake did not mind in the least. Pierre did not seem to hear him at all.

Their more comfortable pace granted Jake the chance to rubberneck. As they drove back through the gradually awakening city, he studied the faces out walking, talking, sweeping, working, filling the cafes, preparing for the day. The streets between the great squares were winding and odoriferous and lined with small shops and tall apartment buildings. The apartments' iron balustrades were often so close overhead that housewives could hand things from one side of the street to the other. The populace was a vivid mixture of races, every face testifying to a melange of Arab and Mediterranean bloodlines. Jake observed, "These people don't look like any I've ever seen before."

Towers nodded his agreement. "Down the centuries, ships from Europe, Africa, and the Orient have dropped anchor here. Countless cultures have left their mark on the land and the people. Yet somehow through it all, the Maltese have remained their own folk." Towers appeared to be enjoying the ride as much as Jake. "The Maltese are strange folks. Never seen much freedom, but they're the most freedom-loving people I've ever known. Can't be more than half a million of them, but they're proud as citizens of the greatest empire on earth. Got to admire people with that kinda spunk."

"There seem to be a lot of churches," Pierre observed.

"Yeah, there's a church for every day of the year, and they're all pretty well used," Towers replied. "Wherever the Maltese go, their God goes with 'em. Their religion is right there in the middle of everything they do. That's another part of the life here that agrees with me."

"I can understand that sentiment perfectly," Pierre murmured, "having seen how they drive."

Towers pointed out his open window at a church they were passing. "This here's the Mosta Church. Three years ago, three bombs landed on the roof during a service. The hall was packed to the gills. Two of the bombs actually bounced off and landed in the courtyard. The other fell through the roof and came to rest in the middle of the congregation. None of the three exploded. Folks call it the Miracle of the Bombs. When you talk to the islanders about the war, this is the first thing they will tell you about. Not about all the bad things that happened, but about their miracle. How can you help but love people like that?"

The hour was proclaimed from churches on almost

every street corner they passed. Several were bomb-damaged, and one Jake saw had no roof. But every-where the people were busy with repairs. A few homes and businesses were decked out with scaffolding, but every church harbored masses of swarming workers. Every church. It touched Jake deeply to see that even their own homes took second place to rebuilding the churches.

When he mentioned it, Towers replied, "Here the churches are not just houses of God. In the local tongue they're called Homes to the Community. Their front veranda and stairs are called the Parish Sitting Room. People come and meet and speak and drink and laugh and court and weave their lives together with each other and with God. When the war ended, the rebuild-ing started on the churches first, almost without dis-cussion. It was just what had to be done."

They left the city behind and began a series of steep climbs through vineyards and orchards and groves of pine and olive trees. The church and its symbols dom-inated both town and country. Around almost every curve was a roadside shrine.

High on a hillside beyond Valletta rose an ancient fortress town. "The city of Mdina, former capital of Malta," Towers said proudly. "The town's over two thousand, six hundred years old. Reputed to be one of the finest walled cities in the world."

They crested the final rise, emerged from a care-fully tended orchard of fragrant pear trees, and passed under great arched portals. The city's outer walls were more than twenty feet thick.

In the morning light, the ancient limestone build-ings shone with the color of champagne, giving the en-tire city a texture all its own. The taxi entered into ways so narrow there was scarcely room for it to pass without climbing the cobblestone curb.

"Streets in these old towns were built winding and narrow so that invaders had no place to mass their forces and could easily get lost," Towers told them. "Folks like it nowadays because most of the town stays shady even at high noon, and the streets funnel the breeze into almost every house, no matter which direction it blows."

They entered a square dominated by a great rose-tinted church. When the taxi halted, Towers unwound his lanky frame and said, "Might as well get out and stretch your legs. I won't be long."

Jake climbed out, eased his back, and took deep drafts of the fragrant air. The loudest noises were the gentle clip-clop of hoofs and the bells on horse-drawn carriages passing across the square.

At the sound of footsteps treading down the church stairs, Jake turned to find Frank Towers leading a gray-haired priest toward them. "Like you gents to meet Father Ian. He's a Brit, or was, but he's been here long enough to call Malta home. Father, let me introduce Colonel Jake Burnes and Major Pierre Servais, late of Germany and Morocco and goodness knows where else."

"Welcome to the Silent City," Father Ian said, walking forward with outstretched hand. "That is the name this town has carried for over two millennia."

"It sure is quiet," Jake agreed. The priest's grip was firm and cool.

"My friend tells me you are in need of sanctuary."

"If it's no trouble," Jake replied. Sanctuary. He liked the sound of that word.

"No trouble at all. The Cathedral of Saint Paul has

been home to wayfaring believers for longer than any of us would care to count." Kindly gray eyes held Jake with a keen gaze. "The place where you stand was reputedly where a man by the name of Publius once had his home. Does that name mean anything to you, Colonel?"

"Please call me Jake." He searched his mind and came up with, "Wasn't he the Roman governor of Malta when Paul was shipwrecked here?"

Father Ian turned and cast a nod back toward Frank Towers. "Very good, very good indeed," he said approvingly. "Frank mentioned that you were a believer. I hope this will add a special flavor to the time you spend here with us."

Towers stepped forward. "I'll be saying my goodbyes here. Got a whole mess of work to do and another shipment due out of here tomorrow morning."

"We can't thank you enough," Pierre said.

"Don't mention it. I'll try to make it back here tonight, just to look in on you boys and make sure you're behaving yourselves." He gave the priest a friendly nod and walked back to the waiting taxi.

"Come." Father Ian gestured toward the church. "Let me show you to your new quarters."

As he led them up the stairs and through the great portico, Father Ian told them, "The apostle Paul was shipwrecked here in A.D. 60 while on his way to Rome. After healing Publius's sick father, Paul declined the governor's hospitality and decided to live with the locals. Many dwelled in the natural caves such as the catacomb under this church. It is said that Paul made his home for a time in the very caves where you will now reside."

The cathedral's interior was vast and domed and

ornately decorated, yet the surroundings held no sense of dominating the people. Smiling, chattering crowds filled the aisles and overflowed into the alcoves, joyously occupied with a variety of tasks. "We have a local festival this evening," Father Ian told them. "You will be most welcome to join us, if you like."

He led them to the front of the nave, through a side portal, and down a flight of steep stone stairs. "Malta is a tiny speck of land, set out in the middle of nowhere, really. The island is only seventeen miles by eight. Blink in a bad storm and you'd miss it entirely. Which makes it even the more miraculous, of course, that Paul managed to beach here. Literally one wave pushing them farther to one direction or the other, and they would have missed landfall entirely and starved or drowned before ever reaching Africa."

The catacombs were enormous, extending out in every direction, a vast series of interconnected caves the size of great halls. Many of the walls were decorated with ancient holy pictures. The electric lighting overhead was one of the few signs of modernity Jake saw.

"Paul had been arrested for spreading a strange new religion in the eastern provinces and had been placed on a ship bound for Rome," Father Ian went on. "In Cyprus he tried to convince the captain to hold over for the spring, as the autumn storm season was already well underway. But the captain decided to go on. The ship was hit by a violent storm and blown hundreds and hundreds of miles off course."

The second chamber they passed through held a great rectory table and perhaps forty or fifty high-backed chairs. Cooking smells wafted in from a side alcove, reminding Jake that it had been a while since he had eaten.

"When Paul and Luke left after their enforced stay, Luke wrote about the regret they felt upon departure, the friendliness of the people, and the many gifts granted them by these simple folk. As a result of this one man, the entire island nation came to believe. And this faith of theirs was not an easy course, let me tell you. After the Roman Empire dissolved about A.D. 500, there was a dark time here. Very dark indeed. The Arabs came and ruled for over eight hundred years. Some of the princes and sultans were good men, others cruel beyond our wildest imaginations. The churches fled underground and hid themselves in caves like the ones here. Finally the Knights of Saint John arrived and the modern era of Maltese history began."

Father Ian stopped before an ancient wooden door. "One of you may take this cell, another the next one along. They are simple quarters, but I hope you will be comfortable. Many of your neighbors observe the rule of silence, so we ask that you reserve your conversations for the dining hall." He smiled warmly. "From the looks of you, I would imagine you both could use some food and rest. We will be serving our midday meal in about half an hour. Please don't hesitate to come find me if there is anything further you require."

Jake spent the day eating and catching up on what felt like weeks without enough rest. The hours passed uncounted, as the caves had neither clocks nor natural lighting. His cell was utterly bare save for a bed, a washstand, and a simple crucifix hung upon the wall.

When the light was extinguished the cell was quiet and dark as a tomb, yet filled with a sense of comfort and peace. Jake felt as though he were surrounded by centuries of prayer.

Then, to his utter astonishment, the peace was shattered by a series of booming explosions. He bolted from his bed, rushed out into the hallway, and confronted a rumpled Pierre, who demanded sleepily, "Are we under attack?"

"I thought somebody told me the war was over," Jake replied.

They raced up the catacomb stairs and entered pandemonium. The church was filled with incense and song and revelry. Above their heads the church bells had begun a bonging chorus.

They pushed their way outside into the night, only to find the entire square filled with shouting, dancing, laughing people. Fireworks flashed and banged high overhead, the obvious source of the explosions. A smiling Father Ian appeared at their side and explained, "Almost every weekend throughout the summer, one of the local parishes celebrates a saint's feast day."

There were bands and bunting and singing and feasting and many expressions of great good cheer among the celebrants. Statues were paraded about. Flowers woven into intricate garlands crowned the brows of some of the most beautiful young girls Jake had ever seen.

"If there's one thing these islanders know how to do, it is enjoy their faith," the priest shouted above the din. "I miss this whenever I return to England. People seem so somber there whenever faith is mentioned. It is almost as though they have been told that you cannot be joyful and religious at the same time. What rub-

bish! We are *commanded* to be joyful. Look at these people. See their smiles, their dancing, their laughter?
They endured as much as any people during the war.
I scarcely know any family who did not suffer the loss
of at least one loved one. And yet look at them! They
are *joyful*.

"That is why I have decided to make Malta my
home. Not just to serve them, but to learn from them.
Twenty years I have been here on this island, and still
I am learning from them the lesson of joyful worship."

Bells sounded continually, and incense wafted upward in great, white, fragrant clouds. There were
fireworks and choirs and processions of lay people
praying and singing and throwing scented water over
the throngs.

"This is not just a carnival," Father Ian told them.
"This is a time of religious thanksgiving. They give
thanks for what has happened in the past year. They
spend almost two hours praying for the coming year—
for health and happiness and prosperity and growth,
never forgetting that last item. Then the festival begins.
This is part of their enjoyment of being Christians and
servants of God on this lovely island."

The priest smiled and turned toward the merry
throng with a gesture of affection. "These, my adopted
people are a people of celebration. They rejoice in their
faith. They see it not in terms of commandments and
do nots, but in terms of victory. They celebrate their
freedom from death. And now more than ever."

It was well after midnight when Frank Towers appeared at the table where they sat surrounded by drink

and food and joyful celebration. He eased himself down, grabbed a chicken leg off a passing platter, took an enormous bite, and waved a yellow paper toward Jake. "This came in a couple of hours ago."

Jake unfolded the flimsy page and read, CANNOT CONFIRM A WALTERS ON EMBASSY STAFF. DO NOT TRY FURTHER COMMUNICATIONS. LINE NOT SECURE.

Jake read it a second time, passed it over to Pierre, and watched as his friend grimaced mightily at the words. "This is not good news."

Frank Towers shrugged his unconcern. "Doesn't deny this Walters fellow is there either, you notice that?"

"What are you saying?"

"Seems to me they're playing it cagey, like maybe they have to, given the circumstances."

Jake struggled to push the noisy festivities out of his mind and concentrate. "So somebody may have intercepted my communication and knows where we are."

"Maybe," Towers conceded. "On the island at least. But look at it this way. There ain't a soul outside of here that knows where you are except me and Father Ian. And there ain't anybody here that knows *who* you are except for us. The good father's got enough secrets to his name to sink this island if he had a mind to. You're as safe here as anywhere."

Jake felt himself relaxing. "What do you suggest we do?"

"Lay low for a while. Both of you look like you could use a year's sleep. I'll be back in three, maybe four days. Soon as I'm back, we'll meet up and work out the next step."

Towers rose to his feet. "Spend a little time on your knees, why don't you? I ain't never found a better place to work through the impossibles in life."

Chapter Seventeen

J ake was so lost in reverie that he did not notice Father Ian until the priest had settled down on the pew beside him. "How are you doing, Colonel?"

"Jake, please."

"Jake, then. No, do not answer that. There is no need. I have watched you these past three days and seen how you seem to drink in the peace here. It shines from your face." Kindly gray eyes rested on him. "I can therefore see how you are."

Jake looked about the splendid ornamentation of the ancient church. "It *is* peaceful here," he agreed. "I've had the feeling I can sort of stop off and lay everything down. Take a little time out from the world."

He hesitated, then confessed, "I've been thinking a lot about a lady I care for. Her work has her back in America, too far away for my liking. Then there's the war; it keeps popping up in my mind. It's almost like this is the first time I've had to really think things through since it all happened. And the desert."

"Yes, your friend has told me a little of what took place during your recent adventures." The priest's voice was gently probing, inviting. "Is there anything you would like to speak with me about?"

It seemed to him then that Jake had been waiting for this question, hoping for it on some level far below that of conscious thought.

"So much happened back there," Jake replied, "and still what I think about most is the silence. At the time, it felt like I was surrounded by noise almost constantly. But the desert's quiet was sort of waiting, always there, whenever the noise stopped, and I could just enter into it."

His eyes searched beyond the church's confines for the memories of treasured dawns, then he went on, "Even here, I find myself missing that special silence."

The priest asked gently, "Do you feel yourself called toward the contemplative life, Jake?"

"I—" Jake struggled to search his heart. "No. I want the silence. I am learning here how important it's become to me. But I don't have the sense that this is where I belong." He turned a troubled gaze toward the priest. "Still, the thought of leaving here and losing all touch with the silence really bothers me."

Father Ian rose from the pew. "Would you care to join me for a little walk? I find some problems can be better resolved when I am moving."

They left the church, walked across the square and down a narrow lane. Father Ian opened a stout iron-studded gate, which revealed a narrow tunnel through the city wall. "This was known as Death's Gate and was once the way earlier inhabitants departed the city for the last time."

Beyond the ancient cemetery stretched a glorious vista of trees and flowers and rock and sea. From their position high on the hill, the entire world appeared ringed by endless blue. A refreshing sea breeze took the bite from the day's heat.

"You may find this surprising to hear coming from a priest who has felt called to a life upon this tiny island," Father Ian told Jake as they walked. "But the Scriptures tell us clearly that true faith does not mean retreating from the world. True faith means confronting whatever the world offers us and seeking God in the midst of it. To do that, however, we must also find a way to move apart from the world, to know God in the quiet.

"In the very first pages of the gospel of Mark, we are told that Jesus went away at dawn and went to a lonely place. We find such references throughout the Scriptures, where in the midst of movement and activity He sought out a time of stillness and silence. All those people would be seeking to hear Him and touch Him and be near Him, and He would withdraw to be alone with the Father.

"In my own studies, I find that there is almost nothing predictable about Christ's teachings. Seldom did He do what was expected. One predictable pattern of His ministry, however, was this regular retreat into solitude, the seeking of a quiet place."

He led Jake over to a bench set upon a rocky precipice. The cliff dropped down to orchards and a tiny village and the sea. Jake settled himself down beside Father Ian, looked out, and felt as though the entire world were there on display for him.

"You as a Christian are called to be led by the Holy Spirit," Father Ian went on. "But unless you make regular room for the quiet, it will not be God who leads you, but people. And pressure. And fears. And the world. Mind you, all these must be attended to. But they should not drive and motivate you."

"I'm not sure I'm strong enough to keep that balance," Jake confessed.

"Of course not," Father Ian agreed. "No one is. Remember, Jake, it is through our weakness that the Lord's power is fully revealed. Here, let me offer you one key that may help you. It is not important that the Lord release you from the events and the circumstances that are causing you all of these pressures. What is important is that you allow Him to release you from the pressure itself."

The priest set his hands on his knees and rocked back and forth. "One of the most difficult burdens I bear is the need to examine people who come to me declaring that they have felt called to a contemplative life. You see, Jake, most people come because they seek to run away from something. But a monk's cell is no escape. Oh no. Far from it. The world can never be totally put aside. What is most troubling to all men is not what they find outside themselves, but rather what they confront within their own hearts and minds."

Butterflies and hummingbirds speckled the rocky promontory with their living rainbows of color, feeding off flowers that seemed to grow from the rock itself. Jake watched them dance lightly upon the wind and felt the priest's words settle in deep. "Then what am I supposed to do?"

"Build an island of quiet within yourself. Remember how, even during the intense pressure of Christ's own life of ministry, He retreated to places of calm and knew moments of sweet release."

Father Ian looked at him with the gentle knowledge of one who had learned the lesson for himself. "The desert gave you a time of quiet, of space, of limitless horizons. You must learn to recognize this as a constant need and seek to carry it with you. Wherever you are, whatever life confronts you with, maintain these moments of solitude. Create a desert within yourself. Hold in your heart this quiet place, where you may retreat and commune with the Father."

Chapter Eighteen

J ake came to full alert without knowing exactly why. He reached for his watch and saw it was still a half hour to the breakfast bell. But something had altered. He felt some subtle shift of the atmosphere that registered on his war-honed senses.

Which was why he was up and dressed when footsteps sounded in the hall outside his cell. Jake stepped to the door, hesitated, wondered what it was that left him feeling the air was as charged as before a thunderstorm.

There was a gentle scratching at this door and a man's voice whispered, "Jake?"

"Frank?"

"Yeah, it's me. Open up."

Jake pulled the door back to reveal Frank Towers grinning broadly. "Now if you ain't a sight for sore eyes. Hope I didn't disturb your beauty sleep."

"I was awake. What's going on?"

"A whole mess of stuff, that's what." He extended a flimsy yellow sheet. "This came for you a couple of hours ago."

Jake accepted the paper and read, TEAVES HERE. SORRY TO BE BEARER OF FURTHER BAD NEWS.

SERVAIS BROTHERS DECLARED OUTLAWS BY
FRENCH GOVERNMENT. REWARD ON THEIR
HEADS. ALSO BUSY THROWING DIRT ON YOUR
GOOD NAME, NEWS OF YOUR DEMISE NOT-
WITHSTANDING. BINGHAM PUBLICLY CRITI-
CIZED FOR HARBORING FUGITIVES. BIG STINK.
SOMEBODY MUST BE SWEATING. YOUR ARRIVAL
IN PARIS MOST CRITICAL. TAKE GREAT CARE.

Jake looked up and observed, "You're incredibly
cheerful for somebody out in the middle of the night
with news like this."

If anything the grin broadened. "I've got my reasons."

"So what do we do now?"

"That's all been worked out." At the sound of footsteps tapping down the stone hallway, Towers chuck-
led. "But before we jump into that, I got somebody here
you might like to give a big howdy."

Frank stepped back, drawing Jake with him. Jake
looked down the corridor to where a smaller figure
stood silhouetted by the dim light. Jake felt the hairs
on the nape of his neck stand upright.

An achingly familiar voice said softly, "Hello, soldier."

His body was frozen to the spot. He whispered,
"Sally?"

Then she was running and flinging herself into his
arms and holding him tight, so tight, so very tight, her
face nestled against his chest and her arms squeezing
him with a force that registered deep inside, down in
the heart's caverns that had remained empty since her
departure. He raised numb arms, touched her back,
her neck, her hair, lowered his face and drank in the
incredibly special fragrance of her. Sally.

The door behind him creaked open. Pierre gasped, then said softly, "Am I dreaming?"

If I am, Jake thought, I don't ever want to wake up, not ever. But the power of speech escaped him just then. He was holding her. She was there in his arms. Sally.

"Stopped by to pay my respects to my fiancee. Her family lives above the shop where you sent the cable," Towers offered, enjoying himself immensely. "And what do you know, but there waiting for me was this lovely lady. Been waiting out there for a good part of the night, hoping somebody might be able to tell her where to find the fellow who sent that message.

Pierre asked for him, "How is this possible?"

"Before we start into all that," Towers replied cheerfully, "maybe we better mosey on back upstairs. We stay here, somebody's bound to come out and have themselves a surefire fit. Can't be more than sixteen dozen rules we're breaking, having y'all wrapped around each other down here."

With a trembling gasp Sally released her hold, grasped his hand, slipped her other arm through his own, leaned on his shoulder, and slowly shook her head back and forth, wiping her eyes over and over on his sleeve. Only then did he realize she was crying.

Together they walked back through the caverns and up the stairs, never for an instant relinquishing their hold upon each other. They walked down the church and through the great portals and entered a world glorying in the splendor of an awakening dawn.

On the church's front steps Jake reveled in another long embrace, then repeated Pierre's question. "How did you get here?"

She breathed deep and sniffled hard and gathered

herself as much as she was able. "Flying in wasn't a problem," she said, her voice still shaky. "Getting you out will be another thing entirely."

"Whole island is buzzing," Towers confirmed brightly. "I've been back less than three hours, and already I've had two people come up and offer to share the reward if I can help them find a pair of renegades recently imported from Morocco."

"Renegades," Jake repeated, and handed Pierre the cable he was still holding.

"Reward," Pierre murmured, reading and shaking his head.

"From what my daddy-in-law-to-be told me," Towers went on, "they got spies and smugglers and all kindsa slimy critters crawling outta the woodwork, all looking for you two. Local police are having themselves a field day, trying to figure out what's going on."

Jake looked down at Sally. "But why, I mean, how—"

"I got tired of writing up reports in triplicate when all I could think of was a certain colonel back in Germany," Sally replied. "I pleaded a case of the never-get-overs, and the general let me go. But when I arrived in Karlsruhe, I heard all kinds of tales about lost brothers and traitors and chases halfway around the world. Were they true?"

"Probably. Some of them, anyway," Jake replied dumbly. Sally. He looked down at the hand still gripped by both of hers. It really was her.

"They were true," Pierre replied for him. "All of them and more. Your Jake is a hero."

"That's not what they were calling you in Paris," she replied, but her gaze was deep and full and only for him.

"Paris," he echoed.

"That's where General Clark sent me. He was the one who filled me in, at least as much as he could. It seems a mysterious letter from Morocco popped up at our Paris embassy."

"Jasmyn's letter?" Jake exclaimed. "Her letter got through?"

Sally nodded. "The embassy heard through Clark's staff that I was back in Germany and got me on the phone and read as much of it to me as I would let them, then I traveled to France and read the rest of it myself. Jasmyn never did manage to explain how she happened to be along on this adventure."

"Long story," Jake said. Her smoky gray eyes were even more beautiful than he remembered.

"Jasmyn is my fiancee," Pierre explained.

"That's what she said." Sally's gaze remained fastened upon Jake. "She called you a hero, too, Jake."

"True," Pierre repeated. "All true."

Down at the base of the stairs someone cleared his throat. Sally glanced behind them, but Jake could not tear his gaze away from her. She turned back, and a look of yearning tenderness filled her eyes and her face. She clung to him once again, with a fierceness that warmed his very bones. "Oh, Jake," she whispered. "When Clark told me the rumors about . . . I wanted the earth to open up and swallow me."

"Miss Anders, ma'am," murmured a voice behind them.

Reluctantly she released Jake and stepped back. "I'm afraid we've got company."

A pair of clear-eyed, blank-faced young men climbed lightly up the church stairs. Their stances were so rigid that even in their civilian garb they looked like picture-book officers. And tough. With one glance Jake knew the pair were as hard as they came.

The first one said, "I'm Lieutenant Akers, sir. This is Lieutenant Slade."

"Gentlemen."

"We're sort of assigned as watchdogs to you and Major Servais, sir."

Pierre demanded, "Do we need watching?"

"Call us guides if you'd rather, sir. Or escorts. We really don't care. Titles don't mean a whole lot in this business."

"I see," Jake said, confused. "And what business are you in?"

"That's not for us to say, sir. I suggest you hold those questions for when we get to Paris."

"If we get there," Pierre muttered.

"When, sir," Akers corrected. "Our job is to make sure it's when and not if."

Sally explained, "They need you back there, Jake, and fast. Things have become very serious."

Akers asked, "Major Servais, I am to inform you that your brother was recovered successfully from Col-ombe-Bechar and is now settled into the garrison hospital on Gibraltar. They got him out just in time, from the looks of things. Big stink about that one, too. Seems Commander Teaves forgot to inform anybody about the little flight he made down to Africa along with a squad of Royal Marines."

"How is he?"

"Not good, I'm afraid. Too weak to talk much. Which is why we need to get you back to Paris with the evidence. You're the only one who's got the infor-mation to set things straight. But the doctors say they think the infection was caught in time and that he has a good chance of making it intact."

Pierre showed his concern only with a deepening of the creases of his face. "And the woman with him?"

"Yessir. She's okay." Akers permitted himself a small smile. "Miss Coltrane is some classy dame, sir."

"They sent me along to make sure you were really who you said you were," Sally explained. "After I twisted their arms a little."

Jake smiled at her and asked, "When are we supposed to move out?"

"Now, sir. If you're ready."

"Now?" Visions of a lingering reunion faded swiftly.

"Time for all that later," Sally said softly, understanding him perfectly. "I promise."

"We were going to try and bring in a transport tomorrow, find some way to sneak you on board," Akers said. "But Captain Towers here has agreed to fly us out this morning, soon as we can stop by Valletta and get off a coded message to Paris."

"Spies and traitors and pretty ladies and sunrise rendezvous," Towers said, and laughed out loud. "I wouldn't have missed this for all the tea in China."

Jake asked, "So what's the plan?"

Towers swung his grin toward Jake. "Believe me, you don't want to know a second sooner than you have to."

"What's that supposed to mean?"

"You'll find out soon enough," Towers promised.

"But—"

"I'm telling you," Towers insisted. "Don't ask."

"Time to be moving out, sir," Akers pressed. "Now."

Chapter Nineteen

They stopped once for refueling at the U.S. military base on Sardinia. They evidently were expected, as they were directed to a quiet corner of the airfield and left utterly alone, save for the fuel truck and a jeep of military police parked beneath the plane's nose.

Jake peered through the pilot's window at the white-helmeted MPs studiously ignoring the plane and asked no one in particular, "What gives?"

"You are strictly persona non grata, sir," Akers replied.

"Monsieur le Ministre Clairmont has panicked," Pierre surmised.

"I wouldn't know anything about that, sir," Akers said. "They just told me to get, and we got."

"You're bound to know something," Jake pressed.

"Not really, sir. Only whatever it is, it's *big*."

The habitually silent Lieutenant Slade added, "Never seen the like of the comings and goings here. Haven't spotted so much brass in one place since we left Washington."

"What were you doing in Washington?" Jake demanded.

"Long story, sir," Slade replied, his features return-ing to poker-faced blankness.

"All we know," Akers went on, changing the sub-ject, "is that we have to get you back to Paris without talking to *any* official. No police, no customs, no mili-tary, not even a postman."

"But why?" Jake asked.

"Sir, if you don't know, then I don't guess anybody on this plane does. All I can say is that you and the major here are a pair of walking powder kegs."

"And just how," Pierre wanted to know, "do you in-tend on bringing us into Paris without some form of clearance?"

"You're headed back into that 'don't ask' territory I was telling you about," Towers warned. "Okay, folks, the fuel truck's done and those Happy Harrys in the jeep are giving us the go sign. Not a moment too soon, either. So just get back to your places and settle down for the ride."

They flew on through the sunset and into the night. Pierre gathered with Towers and Akers and Slade in the cockpit, granting Jake and Sally a semblance of pri-vacy back in the cavernous hold.

Their seats were formed from dusty burlap sacking and canvas straps. The hold was drafty and smelled of oil and dirt and previous cargoes. The ancient plane creaked and groaned and bucked and roared.

Jake had never felt happier or more comfortable in his entire life.

It was far too noisy for conversation, save the oc-casional few words spoken loudly and directly into the other's ear. Words about loving and missing and wanting. The hold was dark save for a single dimly glowing lamp that granted just enough light for them to see each other's eyes if they drew up close, which was how they remained. All else was said with looks and embraces and lips.

Too soon the hold echoed with shouts and movements. Reluctantly Jake released her and rose to his feet, pulling Sally along with him. They walked up to where the others gathered at the back of the cockpit. "What's up?"

Towers turned from his controls and grinned. "You remember that part I said you didn't want to know about? Well, it's done arrived."

"Here, sir," Akers said, thrusting a bulky knapsack toward Jake. "You need to put this on."

Jake looked down at the bundle. "What is this?"

"Showtime, old son," Towers said gaily.

"This is a parachute," Jake said. "What do I need a parachute for?"

"Makes the drop a lot easier to take," Towers replied. "Especially the last part."

Sally moved up close to him. "You wouldn't make me go out there by myself, now would you? Not in the dark."

He looked down at her. "You knew about this?"

"Right from the start, sir," Akers confirmed. "The brass spent a good half hour describing a night drop to her, trying to convince her to give them something they could use to confirm that you were who you said you were. But she wouldn't budge." He looked at Sally and shook his head. "Looks like you and Major Servais both got more than your share of luck in the dame category."

"It wasn't luck," Sally said, her eyes resting on Jake.

"Anything you say, ma'am." Akers adjusted his own chute and said, "Better get a move on, sir. We're at two minutes and counting."

A creak and roar and rush of wind announced the winching down of the back ramp. Pierre moved up to Jake and shouted, "Have you ever jumped before?"

"Not since basic training."

"That's more than I have had. Any advice?"

"Bend your knees before you hit, and stay out of the trees."

"How am I to see trees at night?"

"That's the part I never figured out." Jake turned toward the grinning Towers. "I suppose I should thank you."

"Wait until you're safe and sound and send me a postcard." Towers stuck out his hand. "Good luck, old son."

"You're a true friend, Frank."

"I suppose somebody's paid me a nicer compliment somewhere along the line, but I don't remember when." Towers had a grip as hard as iron. "I'll be praying for you, Jake."

"One minute, sir," Akers pressed. "Chute up."

Jake's fingers fumbled with unfamiliar straps and catches. He watched Akers tighten Sally's rig and followed his example. Together with the others he walked back toward the cold clear night that shone through the aft opening and felt his heart rate surge. He found Sally's hand nestling in his own, glanced at Pierre, found himself trading an idiot's grin.

"Hook on, everybody!" Akers called and connected Sally's clip to the overhead wire. As Jake followed suit, Akers yelled above the roaring slipstream, "Slade goes first, I go last. Five seconds between each person. Ready?"

Sally reached up and planted a final kiss firmly on Jake's lips. She shouted something that the wind whipped away. But the look in her eyes was crystal clear.

"Go! Go!"

Chapter Twenty

The instant of free-fall before his chute opened seemed to go on and on forever. Then there was a great whomping tug on his shoulders, and his view of the stars was suddenly cut off by a huge circular envelope that glowed pale and beautiful in the faint illumination. Jake took a look around, spotted two other chutes within range, hoped one of them was Sally, resisted the urge to call to her.

The ground rushed up impossibly fast, dark and foreboding. Jake found his heart rate surging to an impossibly high pace, his breath coming in explosive little gasps. Shreds of distant training echoed around in his panicking brain. Choose a point, bleed air, stay loose, try to take up a coiled position like a spring ready to bounce.

Then all thought froze, the ground charged up, his feet struck, and he rolled and rolled and bumped and finally stopped. Jake lay completely wrapped up in the cords and the silk, gasping hard, his heart thundering in his ears. He took stock. Everything hurt. His feet and legs and back and arms and shoulders and head. Everything. But he could feel his toes; he had read somewhere that was a good sign. And his fingers moved.

He checked his thighs, found nothing out of the ordinary. And then his breathing eased, and suddenly he found himself laughing.

"Colonel Burnes, is that you, sir?"

"That was great," Jake said. "Just don't ask me to do it again, okay?"

"Anything you say, sir. Hang on and let me cut you loose."

"Where's Sally?"

"Slade's seeing to her."

"And Pierre?"

"Landed like a pro, sir," Akers replied, his voice registering both shock and approval. "By the time I got to him he was already stowing his chute."

Another set of footsteps approached, and Pierre said, "Is that a shroud for the dearly departed colonel, or is he merely having a rest, I wonder."

"Show-off," Jake muttered.

"Perhaps you and I could get together again when this is over," Pierre offered, "and I could give you a few lessons."

"Not on your life." The ropes loosened, and Jake managed to clear the chute from his face. He looked up at a broadly smiling Pierre and asked, "How did you do it?"

"To be perfectly honest, I have no idea. One minute I was up and flying, the next I was standing in this glorious field under this beautiful sky."

"Beginner's luck," Akers said, sawing through the final rope. "Okay, sir. You're clear."

Jake kicked his legs free, scrambled to his feet, and looked over to where another chute lay spread out in the moonlight about a hundred feet away. Something about the scene caught in his throat. He raced over.

Jake fell to his knees beside where Sally sat, with Slade crouching by her legs. "What's the matter?"

"Nothing," Sally snapped, but even in the dim light he could see she was in pain.

"Ankle," Slade said. "Doesn't appear too serious, though. Just a twist or maybe a minor sprain."

"Maybe we should leave you here with the others, ma'am," Akers said, coming up alongside.

"Not a chance," Sally said. "Jake, make them listen to reason. I didn't come this far to miss out on the grand finale."

Jake looked up at Akers. "What others?"

Pierre hissed, crouched, and pointed at the trees bordering their field. Jake squinted, saw a series of shadows separate and begin walking toward them. He was reaching to scoop up Sally when Akers stopped him with, "It's okay, sir. They're some of ours." He straightened and whistled softly. Again.

A slender figure broke away and raced ahead of the others. A familiar voice called out, "Pierre?"

"Jasmyn!" Pierre leapt to his feet and bolted toward her. They came together and embraced and their two shadows became one.

"Like I said, sir," Akers said approvingly. "That's some dame."

Chapter Twenty-One

W e did not fight and sacrifice for our freedom to see it taken away from within."

The gruff-voiced elder was the only one of the group crammed into the back of the ancient transport van who spoke any English. Yet the intensity with which the others listened to his words left no room for doubt that they all felt the same.

"We have always known there were those among us who would climb upon the backs of their country-men, ever hungry for more land, more money, more titles, more power." The elder passed on the flagon without even seeing what moved through his hands. "The tradition of *La Résistance* is as old as France her-self. We have ever had to fight the forces of greed and tyranny. It is the way."

The way. Jake fed hungrily on the fresh-baked bread and crumbly farmer's cheese and ripe early sum-mer apples, taking great bites from each in turn while he pondered what the old man was saying. The way. He listened and heard not only the words, but the same connecting thread he had found in the desert reaches, a world and more away from this rattling van rumbling through the night toward Paris.

Men and women would be ever faced with choices. Their values and actions formed both who they were and the world in which they lived. And those who chose the path of honor would ever be challenged by the fierce crosswinds of those who sought to live for self alone.

Jake suddenly saw that he would be called to stand and defend all he saw as precious—his faith, his land, his way of life. But all he said was, "It is good of you to help us."

"It is an honor to serve with Mademoiselle Coltrane and the brother of Patrique Servais. Even here in the north we have heard of their work. Friends of theirs are friends of ours." Dark eyes glinted beneath brows frosted with the winter winds of age. "And while there is still strength left in this old body, ever will I stand ready to do battle for my beloved country."

"Let us hope it does not come to that," Pierre murmured, his eyes resting upon Jasmyn.

They were all dressed in worker's blue denim, the traditional uniform of the countless denizens who labored at menial tasks throughout all France. Sally and Jake sat squeezed together at the back of the jouncing wheezing van, one of many bringing day laborers into early-morning Paris.

A hiss of warning from the front seat silenced further conversation as they approached the police checkpoint marking the city's outskirts. A pair of blue-caped men opened the back doors, requested papers, inspected each face in turn. Jake glanced at Sally and saw a face smudged and lined with exhaustion and pain, her hair tucked up into her denim cap. Indeed they all looked exhausted, their features matching those of

people bored and sleepy and disgruntled over an uncomfortable daily routine.

The policemen handed back their papers, slammed
the rear doors, and with a belch of smoke the ancient
van trundled on toward Paris.

When the city finally came into view, Pierre
wrenched his gaze from Jasmyn's face to watch the
skyline through the smudged back windows. "It seems
as though my Paris has returned to an earlier age."

"Your Paris?" Jake looked at him. "I thought your
family was from Marseille."

Pierre cast him a haughty glance. "All Frenchmen
may claim Paris as their own. It is part of our birth-
right."

The city did appear to have slipped back into a by-
gone era. Many of the buses and transports were horse-
drawn affairs, rattling along on rickety wooden spin-
dle-wheels and being chased by high-backed jalopies
that passed with bleats from side-mounted brass horns
and winks from the polished lanterns serving as head-
lights. There were so many of these dilapidated vehicles that the occasional modern car seemed out of
place.

"Paris belongs not just to the Parisians," Pierre
went on. "Paris belongs to all France. Paris is the crown
worn by all Frenchmen. One comes to Paris to escape
from the provincial life. One returns to the provinces
to escape from Paris."

"You realize," Jake said, exhilarated by the feeling
that it was all drawing down to the wire, "you're making absolutely no sense whatsoever."

"That's because you're not French," Pierre said
smugly. "There are some things that can be understood
only by one of our—"

"Persuasion?" Jake offered.

"Sensibilities," Pierre corrected.

"You're saying I don't belong?"

"Oh no," Pierre replied, only half mocking. "The fact that you are in love, my friend, makes you welcome here. For all those who love, Paris is their second home. Even when they are not here, Paris remains their second home."

Jake turned his gaze back to the window. The River Seine sparkled and beckoned in the early-morning sunlight. Elms and chestnuts lining the riverbanks spread banners of leafy welcome over their passage. In the distance, the Eiffel Tower rose straight and proud into the glorious blue sky.

"Paris is an enormous experience," Pierre said to the window. Jasmyn watched him with a fond smile of approval brightening her tired features. "It is a city to be seen and touched and tasted and breathed. It is a city made for sunlight, for walking, for laughing, for love."

"I'm all for that." Jake looked down at Sally and felt his heart grow wings at the joy of it all. "You doing okay?"

"You don't need to keep asking me that every five minutes," she replied, but she graced him with a from-the-heart look.

"Heads up, everybody," warned Akers from his seat at the front. "We're beginning the final approach."

They joined the hodgepodge of bicycles and trucks and horse-drawn wagons and buses and cars jamming into a great circular plaza adorned by a lofty Egyptian monolith. "Place de la Concorde," Pierre said. "The new American Embassy is just ahead of us, beside the Hotel du Crillon."

A hiss from the front seat silenced them as the van rumbled around the square and pulled up in front of great iron gates. A cordon of blue-caped policemen flanked a pair of striped barriers. Together with the others, Jake climbed from the van and handed his papers over for a second inspection. He watched the policeman examine the forged documents with his head down and his heart in his throat. But the policeman was tired and bored and had no interest in harassing the morning cleaning crew, especially when their papers bore the official embassy stamp. He shoved the papers back into Jake's hands and waved for the barrier to be raised. Jake walked forward, resisting the urge to offer Sally a helping hand. She walked on beside him with a barely discernible limp, her face set in grimly determined lines.

Once through the first barrier, they came face-to-face with a phalanx of Marines, backed up by a master sergeant with the jaw of an ox and eyes of agate. He cast one lightning glance at Akers and gave the soft order, "Pass 'em all. Now."

They were in.

Chapter Twenty-Two

The embassy still bore remnants of elegance from its former existence as a ducal residence. They walked up the cobblestone path, through the great double doors, and were immediately surrounded by shouting, scurrying activity.

"Colonel Burnes. Here, sir, over this way. You too, Major Servais."

Jake struggled against the arms pulling him forward. "But Sally—"

The young staffer wore a severe dark suit and a white shirt so starched it looked almost blue. "Sir, there's no time. The minister is due here in less than twenty minutes."

Jake wrenched his arm free and halted traffic by simply refusing to budge. "You just hold your horses, mister."

"But sir—"

"Quiet," Jake snapped. He turned back to the denim-clad group standing in the foyer. He searched out the old man who spoke English and told him, "We could not have done this without you."

"Is it true what Mademoiselle Coltrane says?" the

elder demanded. "Your evidence will be enough to end this traitor's quest for power?"

Pierre stepped forward and promised solemnly, "We are going to bury him. Just as he has tried to do to me, my friends, my fiancee, and my brother. His name will be wiped from the pages of history."

"Then it was our duty to help." The elder straightened as much as his years would allow. He raised his work-hardened hand into a salute. Jake and Pierre came to attention and snapped off a reply. "Go with God, messieurs."

Jake turned back to the gaping official and stated flatly, "Miss Anders and Miss Coltrane are to accompany us wherever we are going."

The young man sputtered, "But the ambassador explicitly said—"

"That is an order, mister," Jake snapped.

The young man wilted. "Yessir. This way, gentlemen, ladies."

They were led down a series of halls, up stairs, down another hall, past doorways and empty offices. Jake supported Sally with one arm around her waist and kept his pace to a comfortable speed.

Pierre asked, "Is it not a bit early in the day for you to be having official visitors from the president's cabinet?"

"It was the only time he had available." The staffer was gradually recovering his poise. "The ambassador had to personally request this meeting to get him to come at all. We, ah, that is, the ambassador—"

"I told Clairmont I had news of the greatest importance in regards to two renegade officers," finished a craggy man of strength and height and distinguished features. He walked forward with arm outstretched.

"John Halley, United States Ambassador to France."

"Jake Burnes," he said, releasing Sally in order to accept the firm handshake.

"A pleasure, Colonel, and I mean that sincerely." He turned to Sally and said, "Have you hurt yourself, Miss Anders?"

"It's nothing," Sally replied.

"Ankle," Lieutenant Akers said from behind them. "Twisted it on landing, sir."

"Well, don't say I didn't warn you. Shall I help you to a chair?"

"I can manage, Mister Ambassador. But thank you."

"Not at all. Welcome back." He turned on a courtly smile and finished, "And good work."

He turned to Pierre and extended his hand once more. "And you must be Major Servais."

"Yes, Mister Ambassador. May I present—"

"Miss Coltrane needs no introduction." The dark-suited gentleman possessed a lofty charm. He gave a stiff little bow and said, "It is seldom that my day is graced by two such beautiful and courageous women. Your country owes you a great deal, Miss Coltrane."

"Thank you, Mister Ambassador," Jasmyn said quietly, her regal air only slightly diminished by the denim work suit she was wearing. "But it is these two officers who are the real heroes."

A second gray-haired gentleman appeared in the doorway and stated in a clipped British accent, "Yes, well, now that the niceties have been observed, perhaps we can get down to business."

"Of course." Ambassador Halley motioned toward the second gentleman and said, "May I introduce Sir Charles Rollins, His Majesty's envoy to Paris?"

"Charmed, I am sure." His inspection of their scruffy forms dripped disapproval. With an impatient gesture he plucked an engraved watch from his vest pocket and sighed. "Well, I suppose we don't have the time now to send them off someplace to wash and change into something more appropriate."

"I seriously doubt that the minister will give much thought to their appearance," the ambassador replied gravely. "Especially after he hears what I have to say."

"No, perhaps not." The British envoy snapped his watch closed and peered at Pierre from beneath bushy brows. "Major Servais, do I understand that you carry with you a written testimony of your brother's findings?"

"I do," Pierre replied. "In detail."

"May I see it, please?"

"Of course." Pierre extracted a rumpled and folded sheaf of papers. "They are in French, I am afraid."

"No matter," the envoy said, drawing out a pair of reading spectacles. The gathering was silent for a long moment until the envoy finally lifted his eyes and nodded once. "These will do rather nicely."

"I did not doubt it for an instant," Ambassador Halley replied.

"No, of course not. Still, it is best to be certain before confronting a member of the president's cabinet with an accusation of high treason." Sir Charles permitted himself a frosty smile. "All of you are to be congratulated. Minister Clairmont has proven himself to be a dedicated foe to our efforts to create a unified and strengthened Europe." He turned his gaze toward the American ambassador. "I don't suppose there is any reason not to share the news with them, is there?"

"If anyone deserves to hear it, they do," Ambassa-

dor Halley replied, and gestured through the doorway.
"Why don't we all go in and sit down. Bill, see if you
can rustle up some coffee and sandwiches."

"Right away, sir," the young official said.

The ambassador turned to where Akers and Slade
stood in silent patience. "You gentlemen are a credit to
your service. I imagine you will want to report in to
Mr. Walters. I will be speaking with you later."

"Thank you, sir." With a friendly nod toward Jake
and another at Sally, they turned and walked down the
hall.

"Come in, all of you." They entered a grand salon
redesigned as a small conference room. Beyond the
oval table was a setting of brocade sofas and chairs
gathered about a low coffee table. Once everyone was
seated, Ambassador Halley said, "Why don't you carry
on, Sir Charles."

"Delighted." The portly gentleman leaned forward
and said, "As we speak, our governments are actively
engaged in establishing a new and unified military
force intended to combat future threats to our freedom
and our peace. We hope that this force will be suffi-
ciently strong to stop such disastrous armed conflicts
from ever happening again. Nip such troubles in the
bud, as it were."

"We intend to call it NATO," Ambassador Halley
explained. "The North Atlantic Treaty Organization."

"Yes, and our efforts are being stymied at every
turn by a certain Minister Clairmont," Sir Charles
huffed, "who has rallied about him every isolationist,
Communist, and troublemaker in France."

"He is a power-mad menace," Ambassador Halley
agreed. "But this very same power has made him vir-

tually impossible to dislodge. That's why your information has become so vital."

"Exactly," Sir Charles agreed. "Bring Clairmont down, and we behead the behemoth. Then NATO shall emerge from the drawing boards into reality, and Europe shall be taken one step closer to lasting peace."

"So you see, gentlemen," Ambassador Halley concluded, "the information in your charge had much more weight than the discrediting of just one man for wartime treason."

"Indeed, yes," Sir Charles agreed adamantly. "And this also explains why he was able to draw such widespread support when it appeared you had managed to escape the grasp of his minions in Morocco. Clairmont and his supporters saw their entire house of cards begin to tremble in the sudden winds of change."

The young official appeared in the doorway. "Excuse me, Mister Ambassador, Sir Charles. Minister Clairmont is here."

Instantly the two gentlemen were on their feet, raising the others with a single warning glance. "Show the gentleman in, please."

The first thing Jake noticed were the lips. They were pale and fleshy and formless, as was all of the man. He moved with the boneless grace of a jellyfish. His broad girth was encased in hand-tailored finery, yet nothing could disguise the loose-fleshed flaccidity of a dedicated glutton. With every mincing step on his over-polished shoes, his entire body quivered.

"I do hope there truly is an emergency, Ambassador," he said petulantly. His voice was not high, but rather lacked any tone whatsoever. "It was most inconvenient to make time for this, especially with your insisting that we meet here and not in my own offices."

"I assure you, Minister, that these circumstances fit the word emergency perfectly."

He sniffed his disdain and turned to the British envoy. "I do not recall being informed that you would be joining us today, Sir Charles."

"I took it upon myself to come, Minister, I do hope you will excuse the intrusion. Given the gravity of this situation, I thought both our governments should be represented."

The minister raised a contemptuous eyebrow at the denim-suited four and sniffed a second time. "Don't tell me you have discovered a ring of thieves among your cleaning staff."

The look on Pierre's face turned so murderous that the minister took an involuntary step back. Jake reached one hand over and touched Pierre lightly on the back. He watched his friend force himself back to the relaxed calm of a hungry tiger.

The minister noticed it as well. Nervously he said, "Perhaps we should have security join us for this discussion."

"Minister Clairmont, may I introduce Jasmyn Coltrane, formerly of the French Resistance in Marseille. This is Sally Anders, of my own government's administrative staff."

"Ladies," he murmured in his quietly rasping voice. He cast an uncertain glance up and down their rumpled forms. "If this is your idea of a joke, Ambassador, I assure you I am not amused."

"And this," Ambassador Halley continued with evident relish, "is Major Pierre Servais, commandant of the French garrison at Badenburg. The other gentleman is none other than Colonel Jake Burnes, head of the American military base at Karlsruhe."

The thick folds encasing the minister's small eyes widened noticeably. A tremor began upon those pale fleshy lips and passed through his entire body. He tried to speak, but could utter no sound. His corpulent body gradually folded in upon itself, and he collapsed into the chair behind him.

"Let us make ourselves perfectly clear," Sir Charles said crisply. "Nothing would give me greater pleasure than to turn the information that these gentlemen have brought with them over to the newspapers. I would truly delight in watching you be publicly destroyed."

Another tremor passed through the spineless frame, and the pale lips emitted a faint groan.

"However," Sir Charles went on, "our governments have decreed otherwise. We are gathered here to offer you an alternative. You will today call a press conference and declare your total and unequivocal support for NATO. A week from now, you will retire from all public offices. In return for these actions, we will withhold all evidence and allow you to pass from public view with your good name intact."

A visible rage swept through Pierre. Again Jake reached over and gave his friend a warning tap.

The minister raised his eyes in mute appeal. "There is absolutely no room for maneuvering or negotiation," Ambassador Halley stated in a hard voice. "Take it or leave it."

The corpulent shoulders slumped in abject defeat. "I have no choice," he murmured.

"Indeed not." Sir Charles turned to Ambassador Halley. "Perhaps our esteemed visitors might be excused while we go over the details."

"Good idea." Ambassador Halley turned to Jake and said, "I've reserved four rooms at the Hotel du

Crillon next door. Rest up and have a look around, why don't you. We'll get together again once this matter has died down."

"We don't have any papers," Jake confessed. "Or money."

"And there is the matter of a price on our heads," Pierre said, his gaze not budging from the minister's bald pate, his fury barely contained.

"My assistant will see to your registration. And as to the matter of the warrants for your arrest," Ambassador Halley said, his own cold loathing showing through as he glanced down at the deflated minister, "I'm sure they will be cleared up in a matter of hours."

Jake shook the offered hands, took a firm grasp of Pierre's arm, and led them all toward where the young official stood waiting in the doorway. Farther down the hall, he pulled Pierre to one side. "I was afraid you were going to lose it there for a minute."

"I cannot believe they expect me to let this matter simply fade away," Pierre hissed. "I will not allow it. The life of my brother has been threatened."

"Not to mention our own," Jake added, grinning broadly.

"And my family's honor is at stake," Pierre continued, then looked sharply at his friend. "I see nothing whatsoever that is the least bit humorous about this affair."

"Think for a minute," Jake said, still smiling. "Did they order you to remain bound by this agreement? Or your brother to stay quiet?"

Pierre's eyes narrowed. "What are you saying?"

"Give them their time in the spotlight," Jake replied. "Let them get this NATO agreement down on paper. Who's going to stop you from going to the papers yourself in a couple of months?"

Pierre stood and digested this for a long moment before the furrows rose in a smile that creased his face from chin to forehead. "My friend, the weight of the world has just dropped from my shoulders."

Jake clapped him on the shoulders and steered him around. "Come on, buddy. The ladies are waiting."

Chapter Twenty-Three

Scarcely had they entered the elegant hotel lobby when a gray-suited gentleman approached. "Colonel Burnes, my name is Walters."

"Ah," Pierre said. "The man who was not there."

Mr. Walters kept his gaze on Jake. "I was wondering if I could have a minute of your time."

"I was sort of looking forward to having a bath and putting my feet up for a while," Jake replied.

"This won't take long. Please."

Jake looked at Sally and said, "Why don't you go on up to your room? I'll be along directly."

"Thank you so much." Mr. Walters guided him over to a quiet corner and gestured him into a seat. "Can I offer you something?"

"I'll wait for the others, thanks."

"Then I'll come right to the point." Mr. Walters was a trim, mild man whose appearance was so nondescript he almost went unnoticed. Yet there was a tensile strength to his voice, and his gaze was rapier keen. "I hope you will excuse me for not joining you for your little session with the minister. I vastly prefer others to take the limelight. Such things tend to get in the way of those in my profession. I trust everything went according to plan?"

"As far as I could tell," Jake replied. "Are you a spy?"

"I prefer to consider myself an agent in the service of my country. You are familiar with the Office of Strategic Services?"

"The OSS? Who isn't?"

"We are in the process of disbanding. Our mission, that of helping to win the war, has been accomplished." The gaze bit deep, and the crisply articulating voice did not require volume to hold Jake's attention. "But other conflicts are arising, Colonel Burnes. Other dangers loom on the horizon, threatening both our nation and our way of life."

"Just what are you getting at?"

"We need men like you," Walters responded frankly. "Men who show such a combination of traits as you have during the past few weeks—leadership, the ability to think on one's feet, the capacity to land in alien surroundings and both build allies and accomplish the impossible, absolute trustworthiness in adverse circumstances, and much else."

"I have been living on luck," Jake replied flatly.

"Luck plays a great part in the success of our business," he replied. "We try to prepare ourselves as well as possible, and then choose people who have the proven capacity to make their own luck."

Jake felt like he was being blindsided. "You are asking me to give up command of the Karlsruhe base?"

"Is that the life you would prefer for yourself, Colonel? Riding a desk in Germany, bound by all the rules and regulations of a peacetime army?" Slowly Mr. Walters shook his head. "I think not. You are a man who feeds upon adventure. And that is exactly what I am offering. Along with the opportunity to serve your country in ways that best suit the kind of man you are."

Adventure. Jake felt his heart surge at the call. "Where would I be based?"

"Anywhere the need arises." Mr. Walters rose to his feet. "I think we have said enough for one day. Why don't you think on it, Colonel, and get back to me in a day or so."

Chapter Twenty-Four

The next few days were filled with the wonder of Sally, the glory of Paris, and the delight of being in love.

The streets of the city teemed with life, but people seemed in no hurry to go anywhere. Simply to be there, to sit and stroll and watch and window-shop, was enough. Thin faces framed bright eyes that peered at everything with great intensity, eager to drink it all in, store it up, refill the heart and mind after the long empty war years.

They took the clattering lift up to the top of the Eiffel Tower, climbed the circular stairs in the Arc de Triomphe, held hands walking down the Champs-Elysees, sat for hours over simple meals. They took a horse carriage along the Bois de Boulogne. They leaned over the back railings of overcrowded buses, allowing the other passengers to push them up together, and relished being in a city where kissing in public was a natural part of life. They lazed in sidewalk cafes for uncounted hours, replete with the day's joy. They walked along the Seine, watched the fishermen and the artists and the other lovers, and felt that here indeed was a haven where love was meant to be renewed.

Paris was a city of love, of passion, of memories, of hope for better tomorrows. The peace and tranquility, the excitement and verve, the beauty and the despair, the fashion and the poverty—it all meant so much more to Jake because he shared it with Sally.

It was there on the banks of the Seine, the third morning after their arrival, that Jake led Sally away from Pierre and Jasmyn and the painters and the fishermen, down to where a bench awaited them, poised beside the river's edge and sheltered by two ancient chestnuts.

Sally seemed to know it was an important moment. Her wide eyes were focused upon him, and for once her customary wit had fled to reveal a woman-child who appeared as nervous and solemn as Jake felt.

Jake turned to her and grasped both of her hands as he had planned to do, his heart hammering with the fear and the joy and fullness of the moment. He looked deep into those beautiful smoky eyes and asked with all the love and gentle force he could muster, "I love you, Sally Anders. With all my heart. Will you marry me?"